The Chinese Visitor

The Chinese Visitor

A Novel of Espionage

by JAMES EASTWOOD

Coward-McCann, Inc.
New York

Chapter One

As his car approached Highgate Cemetery, H'an Yang, Special Emissary and Trade Commissioner of Red China, thought benevolently of the people of London, the people of the whole world.

The previous evening he had been met, with proper ceremony, at the airport by Her Britannic Majesty's Secretary of State for Foreign Affairs and had dined at Number 10. He was pleased with the accommodation provided for him at Claridge's and intrigued by the novelty of the famous English breakfast. Indeed, so copiously had he partaken of this breakfast that the only thought troubling his mind at this moment was how to refuse most of the luncheon due in less than two hours at the House of Commons without offending his hosts.

Serene and smiling, H'an Yang slowly sucked a digestive tablet. The talks for which he had come to Britain would, he was sure, proceed with the utmost cordiality.

True, extremist left-wing members of the Party in Peking objected to his mission.

A right-wing organization in Britain had already demonstrated against him.

But the important thing was, he was here! After the latest incident, Russia and the United States were again almost at one another's throats. The moment had come for China to seek allies in the West.

With humility and peace in his heart, H'an Yang, sometime professor of philosophy at the University of Nanking, felt unworthy yet proud that he had been chosen to play a role in the great drama.

At his own request the car stopped at the cemetery gates so that he might complete the pilgrimage on foot. He was accompanied only by his own small entourage and Chinese Embassy staff—his British hosts tactfully absenting themselves from this private occasion.

Karl Marx, after all, had lived in London for the greater part of his life, written *Das Kapital* in the British Museum and nobody had taken much notice of him.

Still, the British had permitted Marx to live, to think, to work. For that H'an Yang was grateful.

The headstones of the graves lined his path in silent ceremony. A lover of trees, H'an Yang admired the poplars. The peace of the scene charmed him, though he found the humid heat of the capital oppressive on this sultry summer day.

The great city lay far below him, endless, veiled by haze, here and there the great new office blocks of glass glittering in the sun. Lazily, a Boeing 707 droned above like a great fly.

H'an Yang was aware that he was discreetly guarded by British police, in and out of uniform. He was also aware of a small crowd of ordinary Londoners, a few of whom, perhaps, were hostile. There were press photographers. Since his arrival he had grown accustomed to smiling into their lenses.

But as he walked the last few yards to the great tomb, H'an Yang became a humble vessel, filled only by the indescribable emotion of the moment.

Stolidly facing away from London, his chunky, stubborn features calm in the faith that came from profound knowledge and wisdom, Marx stared back, it seemed benignly, at his Chinese visitor.

Carved in letters of capitalistic gold on the granite slab,

2

H'an Yang read the words: 'The philosophers have only interpreted the world in various ways. The point, however, is to change it.'

The eyes of the philosopher turned politician filled with tears. His entourage drew back as he placed a small bunch of red carnations at the foot of the tomb—close to a small red banner on which, in faded Gothic German script, was written: '*Der Sozialismus aber lebt und wird siegen*', a tribute no doubt of pilgrims from across the Rhine.

Precisely at the moment H'an Yang, his eyes still moist, drew back from the tomb, the shot came. A single, sharp crack.

Without a sound, the philosopher fell at the foot of his master. Those who rushed to help him saw nothing could be done. In ten seconds he was dead.

Utter confusion. Any one of a hundred tombstones could have concealed the assassin.

Some of the police fanned out in a vain search among the graves. Others tried to control the small crowd, the press photographers, impertinent, probing.

Someone in the crowd began to clap. A scuffle started.

A young policeman, raw, perspiring, helpless, tried to intervene, and had his helmet knocked off. Several youths eluded him.

Then he saw a young woman wearing the kind of clothes he associated with ban-the-bomb political delinquents, and grabbed her. She kicked him decisively in the shins, wriggled and would undoubtedly have got away if another P.C. hadn't come to his aid. An arrest had to be made.

The odd thing was that this particular girl had nothing to do with the demonstration, had been unaware of H'an Yang's intended pilgrimage to Highgate.

She was among the graves simply because she liked visiting cemeteries.

Chapter Two

The Magistrate stared at her opaquely, seeing and not seeing, the face almost featureless, fresh and pink, the only touch of colour in the court-room.

A fat, overgrown schoolboy, she thought, sated by the daily diet of petty theft, drunkenness, trivial motoring offences and prostitution.

For a brief moment the Magistrate imagined himself—for the first time in how many years—a guardian of society, a protector of the ordered British way of life. But the young woman in the dock before him seemed too trivial an antagonist—leather jacket, jeans, unkempt hair, just another sample of her generation. Rather like his own granddaughter.

'Anna Maria Zordan,' he said, wondering at the oddity of the surname. 'I find you guilty of insulting a police officer and resisting arrest. You will go to prison for one week . . .' —he paused—his pauses brought a few touches of what he imagined to be drama to the daily petty tragedies of his court—'. . . or pay a fine of $30.'

He added the option because he was bothered by the image of his granddaughter who had marched in more than one procession, demanding—what was it?—no arms to

4

South Africa. . . . Here before him, but for the grace of God. . . .

'I refuse to pay the fine!'

The voice was fresh and clear, with a slight tremor of nerves, perhaps the merest trace of some indefinable foreign accent. That would explain the surname.

The Magistrate shrugged. 'Very well. If you prefer prison. . . .'

'It's not a question of preference but of principle. . . .'

'You will not use the dock to make political speeches!' The Magistrate cut her short—with a gesture. Suddenly the girl was far too obstreperous to be *his* granddaughter. 'Next case!'

Prison! The word sent a shiver through her body like a man's openly uttered invitation to sex. Direct, uncompromising, and, in this case, impossible to decline. An incredible, but invited, legalized assault on her person.

A tap on her shoulder and she was marching, puppet-like, to the cells.

Riding in the Black Maria, the whole procedure of going to jail, she said afterwards, was one of her most cherished experiences. The stripping, bathing, medical examining— like the enrolment procedure of some nightmarish boarding school. The bang of the cell door, the grate of the key, the feel of a much-worn, much laundered prison dress, rough, after nylon, to the skin. Cocoa. The Bible, read for the first time in years. Lights out. And then the sounds, sometimes sinister, sometimes pathetic, sometimes animal, of the darkened unsleeping jail.

'An absolutely basic modern experience I hadn't had,' Anna explained. 'Arrest, imprisonment, humiliation, the fear of the caged man or woman disintegrating into beast. Things I just didn't know about at first hand.'

'So that's why you did it—got yourself arrested. For a *kick?*'

5

'Not a kick, Ronnie. I was born in 1938. I don't remember the war. I could have been in Auschwitz. But things didn't happen that way. Suppose I'd been a coloured girl at Sharpeville—or Little Rock, Harlem. . . . Oh, I haven't said "thank you" for paying the fine! I wish you hadn't. Not so soon, anyway. In a perverse sort of way, I was enjoying myself.'

Ronnie, who was thirty, worked in the City, had served in a famous regiment and was filthy rich, grimaced at Cleopatra's Needle as the taxi bowled along the Embankment. He said, 'Well, I'm sorry, poppet, but that's one kind of enjoyment you'll have to do without after we're married.'

Anna stared at him. 'That's why you got me out of jail. To propose!'

She burst out laughing. It wasn't a proposal, just a bland assumption. Ronnie had gone down to Holloway in the middle of a bullish morning on the Stock Exchange, to secure the release of a girl who'd picked him up at a party only three weeks ago. Funny. Also touching.

The enormity of the compliment suddenly struck her forcibly. She stopped laughing.

'All right,' Ronnie said. 'Now that's settled, where shall we lunch? Somewhere to suit your dress or mine? Soho or the Caprice?'

'Ronnie,' she said, 'you're delicious as a lover, but you'd be an impossible husband. For me. I'm an egg-head, a scatter-brain, a selfish little bitch who can be devoted to all sorts of lost causes. There are times when I'd do anything to get a man—others when I have to be chaste as a nun. Married, we'd loathe one another in a week.'

She leaned forward, slid the partition and said to the driver, 'Stop here!' in the bright, brittle voice she sometimes affected when she wanted to seem especially detached and efficient.

6

She opened the door. 'Oh, can you lend me a couple of pounds?'

'Take five,' Ronnie opened his notecase.

'Two's plenty.' She kissed him lightly on the cheek. 'Thanks for the kind offer.'

She got out of the cab and marched off towards the Westminster Underground, a neat, provocative figure, trousers tight as a second skin.

Ronnie looked after her with regret. A pity.

Something was wrong. Anna knew it the moment she opened the door of her mews flat. Senses alert, she stood quite still in the diminutive hall. Her nostrils twitched. Cigarette smoke.

Undoubtedly Gauloise. French anyway. Several of her friends smoked them—more chic than American—but none of them, as far as she knew, had a key.

A small thrill of apprehension, almost pleasurable. What to do? Call out 'Who's there?' That struck her as ridiculous, corny. Fetch the police?

Even more absurd. Does a convicted disturber of the peace, released from prison hardly more than an hour ago, call on the powers of law and order for help?

Silently, she slipped off her shoes and crept upstairs, carefully avoiding the boards she knew creaked.

The click of a lighter, the sigh of exhaled tobacco smoke, the clink of glass. The door of the big all-purpose living-, sleeping-, working-, loving-room was slightly ajar.

Anna thrust it wide open.

He was a comfortable-looking man of around 180 pounds, immaculately tailored, cosmopolitan style, perhaps forty-five years old, but his crew-cut made him look younger. He smiled with a set of perfectly white teeth, said, 'You made a lot of noise coming upstairs!'

The accent was Common Market English, German division.

7

He raised his glass, as if in greeting. 'But I forgive anything to a woman who keeps such excellent pot-stilled Scotch.'

Anna looked at the disorder in the room. The open drawers and cupboards, the Braque reproduction aslant on the wall, the carpet rolled back, the records littered around the hi-fi.

Irritated rather than frightened, saying nothing she replaced Bartók's *Concerto for Orchestra* and a Brubeck on the rack. He was saying, 'Whisky—one of the few international institutions whose aims are entirely uncomplicated. Legitimate profit for the distillers, solace for those who drink. You agree? Perhaps you'll join me?'

Anna said, 'Before we continue the party chat, you're sure you're at the right address?'

'Oh, quite sure, Miss Zordan. *Zordan*,' he repeated. 'An old Hungarian name. Right?'

She said nothing, waiting for him to go on.

He said, 'Eight months. I've waited for this meeting. I'm delighted.'

'Why?'

'Because I knew your father.'

Anna stiffened.

'My very close friend. Very close. Sometimes inseparable. I knew your mother, too.' The visitor lit another Gauloise. 'Andreas Zordan, Hungarian. Your mother, American. A marvellous marriage. And remarkable, because international marriages are rather like international treaties ... so much scope for misunderstandings, wilful insistence on differences . . . poof . . . a little puff of wind. Still your father was a diplomat, a cosmopolitan, adaptable—as on the day he walked out of the Hungarian Embassy in London in the early days of the war, and never went back.'

Stung, Anna said, 'My father was anti-Nazi.'

'Oh, naturally, of course. So you're Anna. Born Budapest, 1938. Educated in America and Switzerland. But you still keep up an interest in the old country.' He picked up a volume of poems by Petöfi from the sofa which she had been reading before she went off to Highgate. 'That's nice! Hungarian is still the language of the heart, the blood!'

Anna said, 'Who are you? What do you want here? What do you want with me?'

He smiled, disarmingly. He said, 'Didn't it ever strike you as odd that your parents never encouraged you to live with them? You living here in London, in America, or on the Continent—always at arm's length?'

'My father was always on the move. Hotels, short-term rented apartments.'

'The diplomat turned businessman with innumerable international contacts. The Far East. South America, Europe. Your poor mother! The constant travelling, living out of suitcases. How it must have tired her. How glad she must have been for those last few weeks, staying put, in Vienna!'

Anna gasped. *Vienna!* Suddenly her body shook, as if she had been immersed in icy water, as the terror came screaming back.

The visitor was saying, 'You do, of course, remember Vienna.' And he smiled, and waited, watching her face crumple.

Last winter the snow had fallen early on the Semmering. The temptation to surprise her parents, go ski-ing and see Hans were irresistible. So she had packed a bag and flown to Vienna, without writing, without phoning.

They were pleased to see her. Only afterwards did she realize how nervous, how much older they both seemed. How afraid! They had positively encouraged her to go to the Semmering for the week-end, as if they were planning the assignation, not her.

But nothing really mattered, of course, but Hans. Nothing mattered but two delicious days of thrilling cold and the warm pleasure of the bed.

Came Monday. She and Hans arrived back in the VW at the crumbling old baroque house in the Salmgasse, where her parents rented a flat, a few minutes before noon.

After a week-end of snow and love she was languorously happy. Hans—whom she had first met when he was doing post-graduate work in London—drove off to the University to give a lecture on Pavlov. They arranged to meet that evening for dinner. She waved him good-bye as the VW buzzed away—and never saw him again.

The bell had that echoing, hollow sound that meant no-one-at-home. Perhaps Frau Schlaffer, the cleaning woman, didn't come on Mondays. Perhaps her parents had already gone out for lunch.

But even as she let herself in with her own key, suddenly she knew, from one instant to the next, with a raw, quivering sixth sense, that something horrible, something obscene, had happened.

She did not call out as she crossed the ornate, gilt-encrusted hall—part of the palace that had seen gay doings in the Francis Joseph era. Even the bathroom, walls and ceilings entirely covered with mirrors, had two secret doors that opened only from the outside. Only three days ago, showing her over the place, her father had said that the place fascinated him because it belonged so completely to the world of *Der Rosenkavalier*. In the world of Strauss he was always happiest. . . .

She threw open the white and gold double doors of the salon.

Her father lay back on the sofa, a red stain, like a decoration, in the middle of his immaculate white shirt front.

Her eyes took in the two cups of coffee on the table before him, the brandy glasses, the bottle of his favourite *Bisquit*.

She saw also the cushion of the empty chair facing her father, still hollowed by the guest's posterior.

Then Anna's eyes moved to the door that led to the

kitchen. Her mother's twisted body lay across the threshold. Evidently she had been to fetch some *Sachertorte* for the guest, heard the shot and rushed in. Pieces of cake lay scattered about her. Fragments of the cut-glass plate glittered on the parquet in the hard, bright winter sun.

Motionless, Anna took in the scene as if making a long-exposure picture of it, and as the image of horror fixed itself indelibly on her brain, and she realized this was happening to her, she screamed. A high-pitched animal wail.

She was still screaming when the concierge rushed into the flat two minutes later, and still moaning speechlessly twenty minutes after that when the room was filled with strange men, some in uniform, some not, and then a doctor, whispering to her in Viennese-petting-German as if she were a child, had bared her arm, brushed it with surgical alcohol and she felt the brief, blessed jab of the needle.

In hospital, later still, they asked her questions. But she could tell them nothing—nothing except that she had been for the week-end to the Semmering with Hans.

Two days after that, in the charge of an Englishman she did not know who said his name was Sarratt, she was driven to Schwecat Airport, and put on a plane. She never knew who murdered her parents. Or why.

Except, of course, that it must have been political.

From that moment she hated politics—and politicians, without discrimination, irrespective of nationality, creed or colour. Politics became the ultimate evil. Politics had killed her parents.

From that time also she had taken to visiting graveyards, cemeteries, in any town, any country she happened to be, for assurance that the dead really lived.

Her own parents had been cremated in Vienna. There was no grave.

The visitor was watching her bruised face with the detachment of a vivisectionist.

'Vienna!' she said quietly. 'So it was you!'

He made a gesture as if he had been paid an undeserved compliment, shook his head. He said, 'Fräulein, I came here to spare you pain, not to cause it. That's why I let myself in while you were out. How did I know your address? It was in the papers—your photograph, too. The Highgate business.' He smiled disarmingly. 'You returned a little earlier than expected.'

Anna said, 'What are you looking for?'

'Unfortunately, I don't know. That is, not exactly. Some kind of record—a notebook, perhaps.'

'A record of what?'

'That is a question whose answer will cause you pain.'

'Say it!'

'Very well. Of course you were aware of the real reason for your father's long journeys abroad?'

'He held agencies for British firms manufacturing automation equipment and machine tools.'

The other nodded. 'A useful and probably lucrative cover. Still business wasn't his main interest. He was chiefly concerned with people. People of a very special kind. Refugees. You knew this?'

'I know he tried to help people. We didn't talk about it.'

'Very wise. He was playing a dangerous game in which he did not want his daughter involved. But if we are to find what I am looking for in this flat, we must talk about it now.'

The visitor took another cigarette, his eyes never leaving her face. He said, 'To hundreds of people who escaped from Eastern Europe, your father was the first man to turn to for help. He had connexions, contacts in every country, every continent. He got these unfortunate people jobs, money, help in many, many ways. In return they would do anything for him. Anything . . . .' He took an immaculate linen handkerchief and dabbed his forehead, spreading the scent of cologne. The heat was more oppressive than ever.

12

'Anything?' Anna prompted.

'This, Fräulein, is the painful part. Because of their unimpeachable anti-Communist background—not to mention your father's recommendation—many of the refugees got important jobs all over the Western world in science, industry, even defence. They had access to important people, sometimes to scheduled, top-secret information. Can't you guess what happened—the possibilities opened to your father?'

Anna flushed. Two bright patches of angry colour appeared on her cheeks as if she had been slapped twice, hard. In her bright, brittle voice, she said, 'You're saying he was playing a double game? He helped refugees, then made them pay by forcing them to spy on their adopted countries for the benefit of the U.S.S.R.?'

Still the eyes did not leave her face. 'Not exactly.'

'Then what—exactly?'

'Farther east.'

Anna stared at him incredulously. 'China?'

The other nodded. 'Why the surprise, Fräulein? China aspires to the leadership of the Communist world. In time, perhaps, the whole world. To fit herself for the role she needs a regimented population, a huge army, the bomb. And one thing more. An efficient intelligence service—on a world-wide scale. But here the Chinese have an enormous difficulty. Outside their own country, ingenious, systematic, unscrupulous though they are, the Chinese always *look* like Chinese. They can't change the shape of their features, the colour of their skin. Their tongues have difficulty in getting around European consonants and vowels. No matter how hard they try, they can never pass, never merge with a Western crowd. They're conspicuous—and doing your work inconspicuously is rule number one in espionage. As spies in Western countries, they're practically useless. So. . . .'

'My father recruited a sort of foreign legion of spies on their behalf from among the refugees!'

13

'The logical, correct answer. Where better to look for suitable material than among the men and women who have lost their roots, owe allegiance to no one, those who would listen to any paying proposition . . .?'

Suddenly, something inside Anna snapped. 'Stop it!' she shouted. 'Aren't you forgetting something? Forgetting those people fled to the West to escape tyranny, often at the risk of their lives! A lot of them *did* die. In the sewers under Berlin, with a bullet in their guts a few yards on the wrong side of the wall. In a minefield with limbs torn off on some God-forsaken frontier. They took these risks just to ingratiate themselves with my father so they could spy for Peking?'

'Don't get excited, Fräulein,' the other said gently. 'Try to consider the matter dispassionately. Of course not all the refugees became spies. Perhaps only a tiny minority. Perhaps only twenty, thirty. Then, of course, not all escapes were, or are, as hazardous as you suggest. There have been many carefully stage-managed escapes, as you must know. But as the West stands for freedom, and every successful escape becomes a small, but significant hurray for democracy, those responsible for screening refugees naturally tend to err on the side of credulity.'

Anna dropped her eyes from him. He was satisfied. The seeds of doubt had been sown.

He said, 'Refugees are neither more nor less perfect than anyone else. But they're more vulnerable, and of course the Chinese do pay extremely well. Let me tell you about a certain Rumanian economist who worked for a Wall Street investment consultant. His knowledge of industry in the U.S. was encyclopaedic. He had contacts among tycoons, politicians, government officials. A charming fellow. Came over to the West in '47. As long as he lasted, a most efficient spy.'

'He's dead?'

'Only a few months ago. His car was found at the bottom

14

of a ravine up in Washington State where he was vacation-
ing. It looked like a simple crash. But the police couldn't
understand why he seemed to have been garrotted.'

Anna suddenly became aware of the other's hands. The
fingers were muscular, supple, even artistic. The fingers of a
musician who played, say, the double bass. Except that she
imagined those fingers twisting a knotted rope round the
neck of a man instead of fingering the neck of a big fiddle.
And the sound she heard in her private ear wasn't a base-
line in Brahms, but a hideous, choking scream.

The hands made a deprecating, diminuendo movement.
'He knew he was in danger. Of course. But what could he
do? Go to the police? Hardly. You'll appreciate how he
felt, Fräulein. You know the feeling. Once you start acting
outside the law of a country it's not realistic to expect help
from the law when the going gets rough.'

'So what did he do?'

'Well, one thing he did was to visit an old friend who
was in Europe at the time. Someone he could really talk
to. He felt he had to talk to someone, or he'd go crazy. For
weeks, months, he'd been showing signs of intense emotional
strain. There was talk of him going into a special clinic for
psychiatric cases—the kind of place where they use all kinds
of methods to find out what's troubling a man. Analysis,
truth drugs, hypnosis. Methods that could be very dangerous for the people for whom he really worked. He knew
this. So he went to his friend to ask for advice. His friend in
Vienna!'

Anna said, 'My father?'

The other nodded. 'Briantanu visited him only a few days
before your father was killed. Then he returned to the
States and took that unfortunate vacation in Washington
State.'

For a long moment neither spoke. The visitor rubbed out
his cigarette. He said, 'You are beginning to understand the
situation?'

Anna nodded. 'I understand you want me to think my father was a traitor so that I will be disgusted, hand over to you what you came here for. I also understand that you are a thief, a liar and a filthy, obscene murderer.'

Again the scene in the salon at the Salmgasse came vividly to her mind. This time, however, there was another person present—the man, now seated opposite her, was seated opposite her father, smiling at the thought of *Sachertorte*, a gun in his hand.

She said, 'I think you killed my parents because of what Briantanu had told them.'

The other got up, almost lazily. 'You are a most perceptive young woman, Fräulein. If you know so accurately what happened in the past, perhaps you can tell me what is going to happen now?'

He laced his fingers together, and Anna heard the joints crack. Again it was as if a cold hand had been placed over her heart.

'Of course,' she said, 'now I know all this, you intend to kill me, too.'

The visitor smiled. 'Correct. But not until you have helped me find what I came here for.'

'Why?' Anna said. 'If you are going to kill me, why should I help you?'

'Because there are many ways to die. Some quick, some very slow. If you choose the latter, you will be left here in this flat, quite alone. You will be gagged. You will suffer, physically, mentally, for hours, days.'

He took a chair, pulled it close to her, then sat down so that their knees were almost touching. 'Now, Fräulein, I will tell you as precisely as I can, what it is I want.'

'You're wasting your time.'

'So anxious for pain, Fräulein? Don't be impulsive. Listen. I believe your father made some kind of record of his conversation with Briantanu. Why do I suspect this?

16

Because when I called on your father and he realized the purpose of my visit, he attempted to burn something— rather clumsily, while going through the motions of lighting a cigarette. It was the receipt of a registered package, posted only the previous day, at the *Hauptpostamt*, in Vienna. That, as you correctly surmised, is when I shot him. Unfortunately, there wasn't much left of the receipt— except for your name and the word London. The address was illegible.'

Anna gasped, in spite of her determination to give nothing away.

Involuntarily, for a split second, her eyes darted towards the tape recorder.

'So,' he said, almost casually, 'it was a tape. Thank you, Fräulein. Now, I promise you, this will not hurt. *Nicht ein kleines bisschen.*' The voice reminded her of a German dentist's, whose patient she once was, when he reached for the drill.

This particular practitioner took from under his armpit a gun, a silencer attached to the barrel.

Slowly, Anna rose. 'No. Please, no. . . .' She was surprised and detached to realize that the voice she heard was her own.

He came closer, savouring what he regarded as a proposition. He said, 'If it were not so vital, Fräulein, to make sure that you are never in a position to recognize me again, perhaps we could have come to some close and suitably intimate understanding. I'm sure you would be an interesting playmate. Wild, aggressive, ingenious. I admire such qualities in a woman. Alas. . . .'

He pressed the gun against her breast and with his left hand cupped her chin, utterly confident. His mouth brushed against hers.

Revulsion from contact, even more than fear of death, triggered off what happened then.

Her right knee flew up as if released by a spring, hitting

17

him with all the force of ski-strengthened muscles, full in the stomach.

In the same instant she twisted aside. The gun spat viciously and the mirror over the mantelpiece shattered. Grey-faced, clutching his stomach and calling her bitch, he levelled the gun. Anna's fingers were already round the neck of the half-full bottle of old pot-stilled Highland whisky. She threw it with all her strength.

The bottle crashed against his forehead. He yelped and staggered back, dropping the gun. Blood mingled with whisky on his face, which showed vast incredulity.

He fell back on to the sofa, almost bursting into tears, like a guest who has been unaccountably insulted when drunk. The room reeked of whisky.

Calmly, without haste, Anna bent down and picked up the gun.

She had never handled one before in her life and had only the vaguest idea how it worked. Since it had already been fired once, she assumed the safety-catch was off.

Anna pointed the gun at his stomach, aware that he was muttering, pleading incoherently, in an unintelligible mixture of English and German. He spread his hand, trying to rise.

'This,' Anna said quietly, 'is for mother.' She squeezed the trigger.

In her hand the gun coughed and jerked. The other hunched up, like a man she had once seen with acute appendicitis. Then he stretched up. Anna watched for a moment, then squeezed again, this time pointing the gun a little higher, towards the heart. 'And this is for father.'

The visitor slumped backwards, a trickle of blood seeping from his mouth. His head fell forward.

Anna stood quite motionless for several moments. The gun fell from her fingers. She fled to the bathroom and was violently sick.

Chapter Three

Half an hour later in the drawing-room of a Kensington house a man of about forty-five who walked with a slight limp because of a skilfully-managed artificial leg, sipped his first dry Martini of the evening.

'So she's agin' matrimony!'

'For the moment, anyway.'

'Any young female who can resist you, your millions and your future title must have a will of iron.'

Ronnie said, 'She didn't resist me. On the contrary.'

'And afterwards? No strings?'

'None. In that sense, most unfeminine. She wasn't even grateful when I bailed her out.'

The other grunted non-committally, said, 'Well, thanks for dropping by and making the report. I hope it wasn't too much of a bore.'

'On the contrary,' Ronnie said.

'See yourself out, will you, there's a good chap.'

Alone, the man with the artificial leg was pouring himself a second dry Martini when the phone rang. The number was ex-directory, known only to close friends and a few colleagues. Nevertheless, with a defence mechanism developed over the years, he lifted the receiver, said nothing, waited for the caller to speak.

'Mr Sarratt?' a woman's voice said, after a moment's hesitation, a scared, tightly controlled voice, he didn't at once recognize.

He put on his manservant's voice, refined Cockney. 'Who's calling, please?'

The voice became urgent. 'It's personal. I must speak to Mr Sarratt.'

Then suddenly, he remembered. The voice blurred by sedatives, the shattered, wounded face on that flight from Vienna.

He said, 'This is Mr Sarratt's manservant. Mr Sarratt was just going out. I'll see if I can catch him.'

'Please hurry.'

He waited a moment, then said briskly in his normal rather dry, clipped voice, 'Sarratt here.'

A gasp of relief. 'Oh, Mr Sarratt. This is Anna Zordan.... You remember?'

'Of course. You sound upset. Is anything wrong?'

He heard the quick breathing, the indecision. Then, 'Mr Sarratt, you do remember telling me if ever I needed help or advice . . .'

'You should call me at this number.' He laughed lightly to reassure her. 'It's quite a coincidence, Miss Zordan, but tomorrow I was going to call you. Suppose I come round to your place? In the morning, say eleven?'

'No! I mean, in the ordinary way, tomorrow would be fine. But it's got to be now—tonight.'

'I'm afraid that's impossible. I've a dinner date.'

'Mr Sarratt,' the girl said, very crisp and decisive now, 'there's a dead man in my flat. I was going to call the police. But then I remembered you.'

'I'll be with you in about ten minutes,' he said shortly. 'Yes, I know the address.'

Sarratt cut the connexion, then dialled a Whitehall

number. He said, 'I'm extremely sorry, sir, but something urgent has just come up. My apologies to the Commissioner.'

Ten minutes later, driving his discreet black Rover, he pulled up outside her place in the mews, a backwater recently much tarted up, transformed from dingy chauffeurs', cottages to white, blue and yellow-painted town hide-outs of the younger smart set. Through an open window came laughter, the clink of ice against glass, the sound of Erroll Garner. Evidently whatever had happened at her place hadn't disturbed the normal life of the mews.

He pressed the bell.

Anna answered almost at once. She was very pale. Her mouth, large and full, had just received a new coat of orange lipstick. He liked this. It meant he wouldn't have to deal with hysteria. She was more beautiful than he remembered, more adult.

She said, 'In the living-room.'

Two smells hit him at once. Whisky and burnt powder. The corpse stared at him from the sofa.

'I don't know his name,' Anna said, 'and nothing much about him, except that he's involved in espionage, killed my parents in Vienna, and a man called Briantanu in the U.S.'

At the last name Sarratt glanced at her sharply, but made no comment.

'I haven't looked in his pockets,' she was saying, 'I don't like blood on my hands. Not literally.' She shuddered slightly, and added, 'God! I could use a drink! But knocking him out used up all the whisky.'

Sarratt took in the broken bottle and examined the cut in the dead man's forehead. Anna said, 'That happened when he was trying to kiss and shoot me at the same time.'

He said matter-of-factly, 'You hit him with the bottle, then shot him?'

Anna nodded. 'Twice. With his gun. One shot for each parent.'

Sarratt offered her a cigarette which she refused. 'Tell me exactly what happened, Miss Zordan. From the moment you said good-bye to Ronnie on the Embankment.'

'You know about Ronnie?' She seemed surprised, but not astonished. He liked that, too.

'Yes, I know about Ronnie.' He lit his own cigarette with his old black Zippo lighter, a relic from the Second World War. 'After leaving Ronnie, you came straight here?' He looked around, noticing the evidence of the dead man's search. 'Presumably you found him in the flat. Looking for something?'

'Something he hasn't found.' Carefully, omitting nothing, she told Sarratt everything that had happened.

He listened without comment. When she had finished there was a little silence, then she said, 'Deep down, Mr Sarratt, only one thing bothers me. Which side was my father really on?'

'Ours,' he said. 'And the other side, too. Of necessity.'

'A double agent?'

Sarratt nodded. 'But he was more on our side than theirs. Your father was a good man. He helped a lot of people.'

For a moment, Anna's eyes misted. She said, 'I'm glad.'

'You're not concerned about him?' He gestured towards the corpse.

'Would you be, under the circumstances? But I am concerned about me. You've informed the police?'

'Not yet.'

'I suppose I was a bit too frank with you. They'll charge me with murder. I'll have to plead "diminished responsibility" because of exceptional emotional strain.'

Sarratt made no comment, expertly examined the body. First the clothing. 'Suit from an outfitter in the Dachauerstrasse in Munich. Tie from the Via Veneto, Rome.' He took a large wallet from the inside pocket of the jacket, exposing at the same time the shoulder holster and getting his hands stained with blood.

'I'll get you a Kleenex,' she said, now completely calm.

Sarratt examined the contents of the wallet. 'West German passport.' He flipped the pages and compared the photograph with that of the dead man. 'Otto Hagmann, born Stuttgart, 1922. Representative.'

'Travelling in murder.'

'Diners' Club Card. About $150, a hundred marks, a receipted bill, dated today, from the Cumberland Hotel, Marble Arch, for a stay of seven days, and a return airline ticket to Frankfurt. Flight 247, K.L.M. tonight.' He glanced around. 'No luggage?'

She shook her head. 'Wouldn't he leave it at the K.L.M. Terminal while he paid his visit here?'

'Probably. I'll check.' Sarratt took the handkerchief from his own breast-pocket and with it picked up the gun. 'How many shots?'

'Three. You'll find the first embedded in the wall behind that broken mirror—the other two in him.'

'The gun's interesting,' he said. 'A ·45 of Czech manufacture.' He emptied the magazine. 'Soft-nosed. Very lethal! Very messy.'

It occurred to her that his manner was distinctly unofficial. She said, 'Look, you're Foreign Office, or something, aren't you?'

'Or something,' he said.

'Well, don't you think you ought to hand me over to the police now or *you'll* be in a spot, too. Civil servants are especially vulnerable, aren't they? I'm sorry to have involved you in all this. Of course, I hardly know you, and . . .' She broke off suddenly. 'How do you know about Ronnie?'

'The lure of marriage is an especially dangerous hazard when a woman is being considered for certain professions,' he said blandly. 'Ronnie is, I imagine, a particularly juicy

23

morsel few young women would be able to resist gobbling up.'

Anna stared at him, her full lips parted in astonishment.

'No questions!' Sarratt cut in. 'Not yet. We have to do something about *him*.' The corpse glared at them from the sofa. 'May I use your phone?'

Under the circumstances, the very politeness of his manner seemed ludicrous. 'I'll send for a taxi,' he said, and dialled a number.

'This is Mr Sarratt,' he said then. 'Will you send a man to Number 7, Eve's Mews, S.W. right away? . . . Make it a strong man—tell him to bring a trunk!'

He hung up. 'It's an efficient firm. They won't keep us long.'

Anna stared at him wonderingly. It was now more than an hour since she had pressed the trigger. She had called Sarratt because in Vienna, and afterwards, escorting her back to London, he had seemed genuinely kind and sincere in his offer of help; because he knew how her parents had died. It was he who had visited her in the hospital just off the Park Ring, several times a day, held her hand and helped her bear the horror of that scene in the flat. They had said little. But his presence had been marvellously comforting. By asking him to come now she had expected comfort again—not a deft by-passing of the police. The whole situation was unreal. Yet Sarratt was dealing with it as if removing corpses from young women's mews cottages with the minimum of fuss was a nightly, entirely routine, chore.

'Now,' he said briskly, 'that package you mentioned, the one Hagmann was after.'

Obediently, Anna went over to the rack where she kept the tapes and picked up a spool.

'You're musical?'

'So-so. The three Bs mainly.'

'Strauss?'

'Johann, Oscar or Richard?'

24

'Oh, if we must have *schmaltz*, let's have it in a big way. Richard every time.'

'Then you're in for a treat. The whole of *Der Rosenkavalier*, taped from a performance broadcast by Radio Budapest a few days before my parents were killed.' She laughed defensively. 'Lasts around four hours. No time to play it before the man arrives with the trunk.'

Anna handed him the tape.

'You've played it through?'

The girl hesitated. 'Well, no I haven't.'

'Why not?'

'Well, if you must know, because my father doted on Strauss—Richard, that is—and every moment of the opera from that damned marvellous prelude. . . .' She couldn't go on. 'I'm sorry,' she said, after a moment. 'I haven't eaten much today. They serve a rotten breakfast in Holloway.'

'I'll take it, if you don't mind.' He slipped the tape into his coat pocket. 'Have you any food in the place?'

'I think there's some spaghetti. But frankly I don't feel like that kind of a blow-out.'

'It doesn't do to be too squeamish,' he said. 'Even with a corpse in the house.'

Anna grimaced. 'I didn't mean to sound like a helpless female who just can't cope with blood on the carpet and a body on the sofa.'

'You're not doing badly. The important thing is, you remembered to send for me.'

Was he congratulating her, himself, or merely stating a self-evident fact? Outside in the mews there was the unmistakable rattle of a taxi's diesel. The bell rang.

Sarratt said, 'It is better if the driver doesn't see you. Go into the kitchen. Cook the spaghetti.'

'That's all?'

'For the moment. Hurry up.'

As Anna heated the large pan of salted water, she heard a few muffled, unintelligible words from the living-room,

25

then the sound of furniture being moved. Finally came the bumping of a heavy object being manœuvred down the stairs.

The water was boiling now. Anna eased the spaghetti into the pan, then, as it cooked, listened at the door of the living-room.

Silence. After a moment she opened it.

The room was neatly in order again. Even the sofa cushions had been shaken out. Except for the faint smell of Gauloise and the pot-stilled old Highland whisky, it was as if Hagmann had never been.

Anna went back into the kitchen and opened a tin of tomato purée. To her it looked like congealed blood.

Chapter Four

The Minister, Sarratt reflected, had an unexpected taste in pyjamas. Generally considered to be one of Britain's worst-dressed and therefore most reliable and trustworthy politicians, on the strength of unswerving devotion to democratic reach-me-downs, it came as something of a shock to find him garbed for bed in *couleur de rose*. (At two a.m., the Minister was also rather less unruffled than his usual unflappable pipe-smoking self.) A few moments earlier, while being ushered into the dining-room, Sarratt had heard a querulous female voice muttering to herself in the upper regions, doubtless bewailing the hard fate that had transformed her from the wife of trade union official to wife of Minister in a few short months. The lady, it was commonly known, had not the same head for dizzy heights as her husband, and was hardly ever seen beside him on social occasions.

It was not commonly known—but Sarratt certainly knew —that the Minister found consolation for a somewhat uninspiring home-life with a certain common little blonde who had once been his secretary. . . . No matter. Probably *that* explained the pyjamas, though it was indiscreet to wear them at home!

'Well, Sarratt,' the Minister said, in his no-nonsense Midlands accent, 'it'd better be good, better be worth wakin' me up for in the middle of the night! I bloody well 'ope so!'

William Hobbs made a point of being rude to subordinates, especially to those he suspected of being out of a higher social drawer than himself.

'Well, I personally found it worth staying up for, sir,' Sarratt said.

The Minister gave him a look that said staying up till all hours was part of his job. After all, he was only a sort of glorified policeman. He pointedly neglected to offer a chair, and took one himself at the oak dining-table immediately opposite the china ducks flying forlornly over a cream-tiled fireplace further adorned by a number of china dogs of several shapes and breeds that looked like 'presents from Clacton'.

'Well, get on with it, man!' the Minister rasped. 'I don't mind tellin' you that security's number one topic at tomorrow's Cabinet meeting, an' someone's ears are goin' to burn.'

'Not mine, I hope, sir.'

'Oh, and why not?'

'Because ...' Sarratt hesitated, shrinking from the melodramatic word ... 'the assassin has been found.'

The Minister's jaw sagged in astonishment. 'Found?'

'And killed.'

'You're serious?'

'Perfectly. His name was Otto Hagmann—a professional killer.'

Already the Minister's mind was racing, anticipating the inevitable awkward questions in the House. 'Why killed?' he demanded. 'Just who do you think you people are? Police—*and* judge and executioner, too?' (That was a good phrase he'd certainly have used if *he'd* been in opposition!) 'Couldn't you have taken him alive?'

'Hardly, sir. One of our operators shot in self-defence in a struggle for Hagmann's gun.'

'His own gun?'

'That's how we know he was the killer. The bullets that killed him have exactly the same markings as those that killed H'an Yang. Every gun writes its own prints on every bullet it fires. Using a gadget called a comparison microscope, a ballistic expert can . . . .'

'Yes, yes,' the Minister cut in. 'I used to go to the pictures when I had time. I know all that.' He lit a cigarette without offering one to Sarratt. 'A professional killer? How do you know that?'

'He admitted as much before he was shot.'

'Seems to have been remarkably talkative. He also mentioned the name of his employers?'

'Well, as a matter of fact, sir, he did.' Sarratt reached for one of his own cigarettes and took his time lighting it, rather enjoying the other's impatience. 'I don't have to remind you, sir, that the Chinese, ideologically speaking, are on the war-path—against the Russians *and* the West.'

'Well?'

'Or that they, the Chinese, believe in the inevitability of war as a means of settling the issue between Communism and Capitalism?'

'Yes, yes,' the other said testily. 'But I don't think we have to concern ourselves with such contingencies, possibly in the remote future . . .'

'I think we do, sir. There's evidence to suggest the murder of H'an Yang was an opening shot in something a little more bloody than ideological warfare.'

The Minister crushed out his cigarette. 'Look, Sarratt, let's get one thing clear. The present government of this country stands for open diplomacy, a cards-on-the-table foreign policy. I personally regard the intelligence services as an evil, perhaps a necessary evil; I have yet to be con-

29

vinced of that. But I have not the slightest intention of allowing intelligence to start dictating policy in the hallowed name of security. That clear?'

'Perfectly, sir.'

'I wonder. I'll spell it out for you. On the basis of the murder of one Chinese trade negotiator, I won't have intelligence selling me the idea that it heralds war. One assassination!'

'Like the murder of the Archduke Ferdinand in Sarajevo in 1914?' Sarratt suggested mildly.

'The whole situation is totally different,' the Minister snapped. 'Anyway, I'm not going to launch into an analysis of the origins of the First World War at this hour of the morning.' He took a second cigarette—the pipe, Sarratt reflected, was strictly an advertising prop—part of the image. 'Let's forget theories and get down to facts. You mentioned evidence. What evidence?'

'A tape that's come into our possession, sir.'

'And what secrets does it reveal?'

'At a first hearing nothing but a rather run-of-the-mill performance of *Der Rosenkavalier*, broadcast from Radio Budapest about eight months ago.'

'And at a second hearing?'

'We put the tape through a new gadget we have that can erase a tape and reveal what, if anything, has been recorded underneath—in much the same way that an art expert can remove a cheap and nasty picture to reveal, if you're lucky, an Old Master. Special kind of tape, special kind of unscrambler dreamed up for us by a Decca clerk. Quite a number of our people have been issued with the tape—not the unscramblers, of course. Very useful new piece in the armoury under certain circumstances, as you can imagine.'

The Minister said acidly, '*I* imagine most devices of the kind create more problems than they solve. The more clever bits of gadgetry the more espionage.'

'Still, if we didn't invent them someone else would—or already has,' Sarratt remarked. 'Anyway, that's theory again, isn't it, sir? The point is that under the recording of *Der Rosenkavalier* we unscrambled a conversation between one of our agents, then in Vienna, and one of his contacts. Very interesting.'

Sarratt savoured the other's impatience.

'Well, go on, man.'

'This contact worked for the Chinese—collecting scheduled scientific and industrial information in the United States. But for reasons of his own, he had evidently decided to change sides. Anyway, that's what he said. For substantial remuneration, of course.'

The Minister grimaced his distaste.

'Spies expect to be paid for services rendered, like anyone else.'

'And just what had he to render?'

'Information that the Chinese are opening a campaign of terror and murder against the West—and the Russians.'

'With what object?'

'To create an atmosphere of alarm and distrust—an atmosphere conducive to war. Russia and the West fly at each other's throats, huge areas of the earth's surface are pulverized by the ultimate weapons on both sides. Then, as the radioactive dust clears, China pours her army of millions over what is left of the prostrate enemies. The triumph of Communism is complete.'

The Minister's face for a moment was a brown study. Then he laughed shortly. 'You believe such nonsense?'

'Can we afford not to? It sounds like a Yellow Peril horror story in modern dress—impossible, incredible. Twenty-five years ago who would have thought the Nazi extermination camps could have existed outside a world of nightmare!'

'Of course you've checked with your man—and his contact?'

'No, sir. Unfortunately, they're both dead. Murdered. Eliminated.'

The slight sneering expression vanished from the Minister's face, as if wiped with a cloth. 'Because of the tape?'

'Well, certainly because the contact talked. Our man, an ex-diplomat named Zordan, was shot, together with his wife, in his flat in Vienna—a few hours after the meeting. A big sensation at the time. We played it down. The contact, a Rumanian refugee named Briantanu, was garrotted within hours after his return to the States.'

'And H'an Yang—where does he fit in?'

'Murdered to distract attention from China—and probably because he was a pro-Western moderate they wanted out of the way. The fact is, he was number one on the list.'

'List? What list?'

'Briantanu talked very freely. He believed Zordan was his friend. He gave names. Prominent persons in many countries marked down for elimination. Scientists, generals, admirals, journalists, senators, Members of Parliament— Ministers of the Crown. . . . All people whose untimely death would weaken the West. During the last war the Gestapo had similar lists of people they intended to imprison or eliminate in every country they intended to occupy—including this one.'

The Minister's cheek twitched nervously. For the first time he offered a cigarette to Sarratt. He gave a dry cackle. 'And all these people are going to be murdered, eh? Any dates mentioned?'

'Only three. The assassination of H'an Yang, London, the twenty-third of this month. That went according to schedule. The next, a certain high-ranking American general is to be shot exactly two weeks later. Of course we've already taken steps about that. They seem to have a 'thing' about fourteen day intervals, because the next execution is scheduled for the twenty-first of the following month.'

'And who was named?'

32

'Well, sir, I'm afraid Briantanu mentioned you.'

Sarratt sensed, rather than heard, the door opening behind him. He spun round.

A pale, nondescript woman wearing a faded blue dressing-gown stood on the threshold. Her glance flickered over Sarratt, then rested on her husband.

'William. . . .' Her hands fluttered nervously. 'Are you ill?'

The Minister did look sick. He searched for a handkerchief and dabbed his face. 'No, of course not. Just tired.'

'It's after three.'

'I know. We've almost finished. Go back to bed.'

Aware that the Minister had no intention of introducing his wife, Sarratt studied one of the china doggies on the mantelpiece with elaborate care. The woman still hovered.

'Are you sure you're all right?'

'Quite sure.' Irritably the Minister went to the door to speed her departure.

When they were alone again, Sarratt waited for the Minister to speak, but he seemed to have dried up.

'Don't worry, sir,' Sarratt said then. 'We'll look after you.'

He was aware that he sounded paternal, even patronizing. This did not trouble him. Governments came and went. He had no doubt where the real power lay in the land.

Chapter Five

Again the night had been unbearably, claustrophobically hot. Anna awoke bathed in perspiration, though in summer she generally slept raw. She lay on her back, eyes still closed, trying to recall the nightmare whose mounting terror had shocked her into wakefulness. But no images remained, only the memory of fear. Then, suddenly, she became aware that the phone was ringing.

Anna rolled out of bed wearing the single rumpled sheet as an improvised dressing-gown. Her head ached abominably. Three nembutals taken immediately after the scarcely touched spaghetti. Barbiturate hangover.

'Miss Zordan?' The male voice at the other end of the line was smooth, faintly transatlantic. 'Miss Anna Zordan?'

'Speaking.' The word came as an almost, inaudible dry croak.

'Miss Zordan, the actress?' The voice was now tinged with doubt.

Anna cleared her throat. 'That's right. I'm not very good at voice production this morning. You woke me up.'

'Oh? I'm sorry! But it is after eleven.' A small, deprecating laugh. 'Miss Zordan, my name's Giltin, Max Giltin, an executive of Target Films. You've heard of us, of course.'

Anna was on the point of saying that she had never heard of Target Films, which was the truth, when the natural desire of a young, unarrived actress to please reasserted itself. She said, 'Well, the name is familiar. But I've never worked for you.'

'That's right Miss Zordan, and it's something we want to take care of. We've been looking through *Spotlight* and it seems you have just the kind of face we're looking for in a modest little production we're casting right now. Interested?'

'Well, of course. Can you give me some details?'

'Don't you think it better to have a face-to-face chat, Miss Zordan? Anyway, we'd like to give you a little camera test. Would you be available in, say, about an hour?'

'I'll have to check with my agent first, Mr Giltin.'

'Why, of course, Miss Zordan, but I've already spoken to him. In fact he told me where to find you. He'll say okay. We'll send a car.'

The phone went dead.

Almost the same moment she hung up, it rang again.

'Anna?' It was her agent, Bill Kraster. He sounded excited. 'You talked to Target?'

'Who are they, anyway?'

'Smallish outfit, but up-and-coming, apparently. If your test's okay it means a part in a feature. Some kind of co-production deal. U.S.–Anglo–Greek. Giltin wasn't too specific, but at the money who cares?'

'What money?'

Bill laughed, pleased with himself. 'I said your rate was three hundred a week. Three hundred a week! And he said "Okay". Just like that.' Bill waited for effusive thanks—in vain!

Out of acting Anna had never received more than seventy-five dollars a week in her life—for one-line parts, or simply wearing a trusting smile while holding the magic packet in commercials.

'I don't get it,' she said. 'Who am I? Who pays Miss Nobody three hundred a week?'

'Don't talk like that,' Bill expostulated. 'How many times do I have to tell you: in this game, or any other, people take you strictly at your own valuation of yourself. And don't forget it! Anyway, for a discharged prisoner, you're lucky to get a job at all! How was Holloway?'

'Lousy but interesting. Bill, you're a lamb! Thanks. I'll be in touch.'

'Look pretty,' Bill said. 'Something revealing. They asked particularly about your figure.'

'They should see me now!'

Anna dropped the sheet and went into the bathroom. Five minutes under first a tepid, then an ice-cold shower drove away the last of the barbiturate hangover. Without drying herself, she slipped into a towelling gown, her skin now icy to the touch. Unexpectedly, she felt hungry. Tomato juice, two soft-boiled eggs and coffee stopped that.

Tossing aside the dressing-gown, she contemplated herself in the large mirror that faced the bed. Her figure had no need of foundation garments, but producers, she knew, had a thing about upstanding bosoms, so, contrary to her habit, she decided to wear a bra. For the rest, panties, just-above-knee nylons, flattie shoes, and a Mary Quant pinafore dress. Very little make-up, a wisp of orange lipstick, hair brushed out to touch her shoulders and partly cover one cheek. Total calculated effect: sexy, but intelligent. She hoped!

The car—a shabby old Humber Snipe—arrived in one hour exactly, driven by a youth with a TV personality haircut, wearing a leather jacket and jeans. He looked her up and down appraisingly in a way that said cowboy, and, evidently satisfied, opened the near-side front door.

'I'll ride in the back,' Anna said.

'Suit yourself.' He transferred the gum he was chewing from one side of his mouth to the other.

The car had a partition, Anna was glad to see, making conversation difficult. She wasn't a snob, but approaches, especially at noon, on the sexual level, irritated her. She was a late-in-the-day starter—a night person.

The youth drove expertly through the heavy midday traffic—south, across the river, to Clapham Common, then the labyrinthine seediness of the South Circular Road.

For the first half-hour Anna simply relaxed against the cushions, just trying to feel pleased at the prospect of working again. It occurred to her that perhaps she ought to have phoned Sarratt to find out how the land lay between her and the corpse. But she hadn't been arrested, and for the moment that was enough. At the thought of Holloway again she shuddered. This apart, she was still on edge. Why?

She saw the youth watching her in the driving mirror. He was, she supposed, good-looking in an unwashed, scruffy way. If she had met him socially. . . .

Then, suddenly, it hit her. There were no studios in south-east London.

Anna leaned forward and slid the partition.

'Just where are you taking me?'

The youth took his time replying. 'The studio.'

'But where is it? There aren't any studios round here.'

He manœuvred the gum round his lower lip. 'Who said it was round here? Another hour. In a very nice bit of Kent, very quiet, very healthy.'

Slightly reassured, Anna regretted not taking the front seat. Comparatively lowly studio employees were often mines of information about the higher ups. She had missed a good opportunity to find out something about Target Films and Max Giltin.

'The studio's new?'

'Sort of.'

The youth switched on the radio. There were two speakers—one in the front, one in the back. Pop, which she

37

loathed, almost burst her ear-drums. Anna found the switch and turned her speaker off, then closed the partition. Beside her on the seat was a copy of that day's *Telegraph*. She leafed through it. No mention of her little murder. The killing of H'an Yang—now four days old—had been relegated below the fold but was still front page. Scotland Yard were still baffled by the assassination of the Chinese trade negotiator. Was it the work of a single fanatic—or was there deeper political motivation? . . .

Freed now from the heavy metropolitan traffic the car was approaching Rochester. The blue signs announcing the M2 motorway came up. 'Get in Lane.'

The youth slid the partition and, watching her through the interior mirror, offered a pack of cigarettes over his shoulder.

'No thanks. I don't!'

She smiled at the watching eyes. No smile came back. They hardened.

'Snooty?'

'I'm not being snooty. I really don't.' She widened the smile.

The youth withdrew the pack of cigarettes and fumbled in the inside pocket of his leather jacket. He produced a small paper bag.

'Prove it.'

'Prove what?'

'You're not snooty. Have a sweet.'

Over his shoulder, he thrust the paper bag towards her.

Anna hesitated. She loathed sweets, but these at least were wrapped. 'Well, all right. Thanks.'

She unwrapped the sweet and put it into her mouth, the eyes watching her—flicking between her and the road ahead. Suddenly, as her tongue got to work on the sweet, the eyes smiled.

'Okay?'

'M'mm. Fine!'

In fact, it was awful. One of those revolting sticky things, filled with an effervescent powder that burst into foam in the mouth. Doggedly, she swallowed the beastly stuff.

The car tore down the long hill and on to the bridge spanning the Medway. The youth could drive. Vigilant, smooth, relaxed. The needle flickering on eighty, passing everything on the road, he stayed in the outside lane until an Aston coming up behind at well over the ton flashed its headlights. Then, surprisingly, he pulled over promptly. Leather jacket had seemed to Anna the type who regarded the fast lane as his personal property.

Speed didn't bother Anna. Only slow, incompetent drivers. In a hypnotic blur the gentle Kent countryside of hopfields and orchards slid past.

Suddenly, unaccountably, not unpleasantly, Anna felt drowsy—and slept.

Chapter Six

'And your politics—in a nutshell?'

Anna smiled. 'Enough to eat for everyone. Freedom.'

'Of thought?'

'Certainly.'

'And action?'

'Provided no one gets hurt.'

'You don't like hurting people?'

Anna hesitated.

'Answer the question, Miss Zordan.'

'There have been times—once or twice . . .'

'Describe them.'

'Well, once when I was at school—boarding school in Switzerland—a girl led a sort of campaign against a friend of mine. She just hated her . . . I don't know why. . . .'

The inquisitor cut in, 'That isn't quite true, is it, Miss Zordan?'

'No.'

'Why did this girl hate your friend?'

'Because she had loved her once, if you see what I mean.'

'No, I don't see. What do you mean, Miss Zordan?'

'The girl was a Lesbian. My friend, Jeanette, wasn't.'

'I see. What happened?'

'When Jeanette told her to find another playmate she became nasty . . . made fun of her, ridiculed her, accused her c f having a crush on one of the teachers. . . .'

'And had she?'

'No.'

'Go on.'

'Because of this girl's reign of terror, Jeanette's life became unbearable. She said everything would be different if only Jeanette would just once go to her room. It was a very expensive school. We all had our own rooms, except a few girls who shared. Jeanette and I shared. . . . Jeanette cried herself to sleep most nights. She became a nervous wreck. Things got worse—so bad that when someone lost a gold wristwatch near the swimming pool, the girl began hinting that Jeanette had stolen it. "I'll report you," she said, "if you don't come to my room. Tonight!"'

Anna broke off, looked around the perfectly plain room. White-distempered walls, a divan, a desk, chest-of-drawers, a couple of chairs, on one of which she was sitting. Plain, polished wooden floor. The window faced her. But there was no view. There was no view because the glass was opaque—and bullet-proof, though Anna did not know this yet. The smell was astringent, like a hospital.

'Why don't you go on with the story, Miss Zordan? What are you thinking about?'

'Oh, I'm sorry,' Anna smiled politely. 'I was thinking that the rooms at school were rather like this. You know—institutional.' The smile became a slightly puzzled frown. 'You've not taken me back there, have you? I'm not back at school?' Suddenly, she was scared.

'No,' the inquisitor reassured her, 'you're not back at school. You're just telling us what happened there.'

'Us? I thought there was just one of you.'

'Don't look round, Miss Zordan. Relax. Go on with the story.'

41

Anna did relax, but now she wasn't as completely relaxed as before. Her voice sounded a little high and breathless.

'Oh yes—well, Jeanette was supposed to go to her room. But she didn't go. *I* went instead.'

Anna laughed briefly. The inquisitor waited.

'The door wasn't locked of course, and it was completely dark inside. I was wearing just my nightie and dressing-gown. Nothing on my feet. There wasn't a sound, but I could sense Hilde listening, waiting. Her name was Hilde. I didn't tell you that, did I?'

'No. It's not important.'

'I walked towards where I knew the bed was and I felt the air move as she lifted the sheet aside for me, or rather, for Jeanette. I stood waiting for a moment, trying to esti-mate just where her face lay. I hoped she'd say something—just one word—so that I could be sure. But she didn't. The conquered had come to offer tribute, unconditional sur-render. I moved to the very edge of the bed so that I touched it with my knees. Then I struck down to where I guessed the face would be. Bull's-eye! Right on target! I caught her cheek so hard the palm of my hand tingled. I heard her gasp. I hissed, "Leave Jeanette alone!" and struck out again. This time she must have sensed the blow coming. She grabbed my wrist, twisted it and at the same time got up on to the bed. We fought like wild-cats, rolling on the bed, on the floor, making almost no noise. Expulsion for both of us if we'd been found out. What I'd forgotten before setting out to right Jeanette's wrongs was that Hilde was an expert skier, played an incredibly fast game of squash, and took gym seriously. Also, she weighed about 15 pounds more than me. A real he-man girl! So, though I fought her till I couldn't move with exhaustion . . .' Anna shrugged and gave a little helpless movement of the hands.

'Hilde won?'

'Hilde won! As she put it, "If you're present instead of Jeanette, fine! As a matter of fact, *liebchen*, I've admired you

42

for some time! You make an excellent substitute! *Ausge-zeichnet!*" Did I tell you Hilde was Swiss?'

'No. That's not important either.'

Anna heard the click of his lighter as the inquisitor took a cigarette.

'Of course,' she said. 'I've never told anyone this before.'

'Of course not.'

'Not even the boy friend I had in Vienna who was training to be a psychiatrist. I'm sure he would have found it interesting.'

'Why do you say that?'

'Well, *why* was I Jeanette's good friend? *Why* did I really go to Hilde's room?'

'Yes. I see what you mean. Have you decided on the answers?'

Anna shook her head.

'Perhaps you were simply curious?'

'About what being loved by a woman was like?'

'Did you go to Hilde's room again?'

'No.'

'But you considered doing so?'

'Not seriously. But it was an interesting experience.'

'And pleasurable?'

'Yes. But not as pleasant as going to bed with a man.'

'You were not a virgin at the time?'

'No. During the holidays there had been a boy. . . .'

'Not entirely satisfactory?'

'Is the first time ever?'

'But the second and third?'

'I learnt a lot.'

'And you've never been intimate with a girl since?'

'No. Never.'

'But you've been tempted?'

'Not seriously.'

'So the incident had no long-term effects?'

'Oh, yes.'

'Indeed?'

'After that defeat I took up judo.'

The inquisitor smiled. 'To make sure it wouldn't happen again?'

'I just don't like being beaten.'

The inquisitor did not press the matter.

Anna went on: 'We were talking about whether I had ever enjoyed hurting anyone. I enjoyed hitting Hilde. The second time was when I shot Hagmann. I suppose I could have killed him outright. But I didn't. I must have enjoyed hurting him—for a split second anyway. . . .'

'A Communist? No. That doesn't necessarily mean I'm pro-American.'

'Are you pro-British?'

'I carry a British passport.'

'Answer the question.'

'Well, put it this way. I *like* England, and quite a few of the English. If I happened to be in trouble of any kind, I think I'd rather be in trouble here than in most other countries I can think of. You know, fair play, and all the rest of it. . . .'

'Still, you have reservations?'

'I enjoy living. If possible, dangerously. When I'm in England, I try to act—that's a risky business. Every now and then I become involved with men—that's dangerous, too. I drive fast cars. I've taken up gliding, and I've made half a dozen parachute jumps. Otherwise, I find life in Britain a bit dull. I suppose it's the lack of sun. I love the warmer sun—the real heat that warms the body and soul, through and through, bringing out the passions, good and bad. But that said, England is a wonderful country to come back to—if you see what I mean?'

The lighter clicked again. 'What exactly were you doing in Highgate Cemetery?'

'Walking. Sight-seeing. I'd never been there before.

44

When I'm in England I spend a lot of time just wandering around, anywhere, everywhere. I love London—especially the secret, out-of-the-way bits. That day I was having a look at Highgate. Burial-places interest me—the pyramids, catacombs, Père Lachaise, Highgate Cemetery. . . . The most chilling I know is the tomb of Edward Gibbon in the Sheffield family mausoleum in the village church at Fletching.'

'Miss Zordan,' the inquisitor cut in, a little impatiently, 'was it by chance that you were in Highgate Cemetery that particular afternoon?'

'You're not interested in the last resting place of the man who wrote *The Decline and Fall?*'

'No. Answer the question.'

'I went there because I'd never seen Karl Marx's grave. Just curiosity.'

'What part did you play in H'an Yang's murder?'

'What did you say?'

'Keep facing front, Miss Zordan. I said: What part did you play in the murder?'

'That's what I thought you said. Don't be ridiculous!'

'But you are, or were, connected with the Fascist League?'

'That's even more ridiculous. They disgust me.'

'Doesn't being a spy disgust you?'

Anna said, 'If I were a spy—which I'm not—it wouldn't disgust me.'

'Why not?'

'Because I have a reason for most things I do. Serious things. And I'd be very serious about being a spy. I think I'd rather enjoy it.'

The inquisitor took a now rather crumpled handkerchief from his pocket and dabbed his damp forehead. It had been a long session. Wearing. More wearing on him than the interrogated. They often appeared to be enjoying themselves. And why not? Complete honesty was a luxury—obviously to be enjoyed.

At this moment Anna Zordan was smiling a secret smile.

45

The inquisitor saw the smile reflected in the carefully placed mirror.

Why a *secret* smile? Was a last shred of gauze left? Even now, after months of experiment, was it possible the technique and the stuff they'd injected wasn't one hundred per cent reliable? Could a particularly strong-willed or intelligent or physically tough subject hold something back? Was the secret smile a mocking smile?

The inquisitor lit the last cigarette in the pack.

'Miss Zordan,' he said patiently, 'what do you find so amusing?'

'Nothing!' The voice was bright, relaxed, without guile. 'I'm just a happy person.'

The inquisitor moved to a small button near the light switch and pressed it.

'It's time for you to go to the studio.'

'The studio?'

She sounded puzzled. Memories of the very recent past were often the vaguest. Memories of painful incidents in adolescence were generally the most accessible. That was how the technique differed most from psychoanalysis—apart, of course, from the time it took to get results, which was minutes and hours, instead of months and years. The psychiatrist was after infant traumas. Still, that didn't stop some of the members of the unit calling the technique 'instant analysis'. Unscientific. But the important thing was that it worked—if six months' experience was anything to go by.

The session over, the inquisitor began to relax. Six months ago he had been a Cambridge don, a sociable one. Parties, common-room chat, congenial people always around when the day's work was done. But this place! It was like working in a mental institution. For the criminally insane. Locked doors. Guard dogs. Special chits even to spend an evening of perfectly innocent relaxation in London. *Quis custodiet ipsos custodes*, indeed! Suspicion and security were his daily bread. Sometimes he even wondered why he'd taken the job. . . . Abruptly the inquisitor short-circuited that train of thought. Heresy.

The door, unlocked from the outside, opened noiselessly. Huett, the security man from the studio department, wearing the inevitable crumpled sports jacket and flannel bags which were the uniform of his section, stood on the threshold. Nondescript, fortyish, like a not very promotion-worthy P.C. on his day off, Huett said in his fatherly way, 'Good afternoon, Miss. Now would you mind coming along with me?'

Anna rose at once, smiling. 'Of course.' She turned to the inquisitor. 'I enjoyed our talk.' Solemnly, she offered her hand. The inquisitor took it.

'Good-bye, Miss Zordan!'

It really was good-bye. Chance apart, he probably never would see her again—another strict 'company' rule. A pity. For the greater part of the session she had been seated with her back to him. Now, quite suddenly, he was aware of her as a woman, a feminine being. The piquant face with the long lashes and orange-stained lips, the smoky black hair that fell almost to her shoulders. Even her perfume, discreetly amoral, he noticed for the first time. As he watched her walk away with Huett down the long, white-painted featureless corridor, he observed her figure for the first time too.

The inquisitor was young enough, and old enough, to feel acute regret for things that could never be.

Nothing mattered. Words, instructions, questions came to her clearly, perfectly understood—and her replies and responses were equally prompt and precise. Yet it was all as if it were happening to someone else. Someone else was speaking, someone else's limbs moved.

She was photographed as she had never been photographed before. Seated, standing. Walking, running. In medium shot and enormous close-up. They photographed her with her hair coiled up and hanging down to her shoulders. They took shots of her wearing a blonde wig.

They photographed her wearing a skirt, then trousers. Then evening dress. They had shots of her wearing the briefest bikini.

The girl as a person, an individual, having been committed to film, she was then reduced to component parts. Hands, feet, nose, mouth, ears—especially the ears, which even the most skilful of plastic surgeons find it impossible to disguise—were subjected to the stare of the camera lens.

Through it all, Anna smiled with unconcern—except, of course, when she was ordered to frown, to look serious, to snarl, to show anger, curiosity, or naked fear.

A woman with the white coat and matter-of-fact brusqueness of a hospital person, supervised the costume changes behind a screen in one corner of the studio. She spoke with a Scottish accent, and the camera crew addressed her as Mrs Bee. And as she had helped Anna into about the sixth costume change, Anna laughed and said, 'Busy bee, busy bee!' thinking it funny. Not a muscle on Mrs Bee's unrouged, well-scrubbed face as much as twitched.

Anna's performance was directed by a youngish man of about thirty-five. He spoke with a slightly familiar transatlantic accent. The camera operator called him Max, and the focus puller Mr Giltin, and in a vague way these two names together seemed to ring a bell, but she neither knew nor cared where she had heard them before.

Shooting took place with the minimum of talk, as if everyone were following a well-oiled routine. Most of the talking, when it came, was done by Anna—into a live microphone.

They handed her texts, not very topical news bulletins containing a fair number of technical terms—from atomic physics, aeronautics, ballistics, biology, chemistry—and ordered her to read them at sight, without rehearsal. And in five languages. English, French, German, Italian and Hun-

garian. The text in English she was ordered to r
the second time with an American accent. . . .

In the middle of the American reading A
feel drowsy. The feeling of calm, amused hap
filled her for the last three, or was it four, h
suddenly as if it had emanated from a light burn
middle of her head which had simply been turned off.

A brief sensation of dizziness, falling. . . . Then blackness,
profound, infinite, in which she gasped and wallowed, her
lungs bursting, as if she were at the bottom of the sea. . . .

Chapter Seven

One European country, possessed of an uncertain climate, unfriendly inhabitants, uneatable food, a hostile government and several million mosquitoes to form a reception committee on the marshy coastal strip—a country absolutely ripe, in fact, for development as a tourist paradise—is not so much as mentioned in a single glossy brochure of even the most enterprising of travel agents.

Only a few hours by steamer across the Adriatic from Italy, which has been making a comfortable living out of the goggle-eyed foreigner for centuries, sharing a land frontier with Greece, a hot contender in the international tourist rat-race, and also with Yugoslavia, a late but ambitious starter, Albania remains as remote from the rest of Europe as the mountains of the moon or Tibet.

Tirana, the capital, is never called on the public address systems of the world's airports. No Western shipping line lists Durazzo, the only decent harbour, as a regular, or even intermittent port of call.

Albania, by order of its government, is closed to the tourist, almost inaccessible to the businessman. The Albanians don't like gravy? They don't want washing machines, refrigerators, trading stamps? Ask them, and they won't know what you're talking about. But the government does. The government believes in the pure milk of Marxist kindness. According to Stalin. According to Mao Tse-tung. Who says? Ask Peking. Peking doesn't have many men in Havana, or anywhere else in the Western world. But it does have several hundreds in Tirana.

Albania, in this year of grace, is China's outpost, her listening base, her little bit of territory, about seventeen and a half thousand square miles of it, in a suspicious Western world.

Getting into Albania is either difficult, impossible, or unheard of—according to who you are, what you are, and why you should be so eccentric, perverse or subverse, as to attempt so apparently unrewarding an enterprise.

For certain people, however, it is comparatively easy.

One of these was Edwin Steiner, American citizen, cultural do-gooder, businessman and spy, now seated on a café terrace in Kerkira on the island of Corfu, with Albania only a few kilometres away.

Steiner was waiting for the contact, the one who would arrange a passage across the Straits. Who it would be, he had no idea.

There was nothing furtive about Steiner. Pushing forty-five, attired in the regulation light-weight suit of the itinerant American, wearing tinted gold-rimmed glasses, with a regulation 35-mm. Japanese camera, plus attendant light meters and filters slung about his neck, and exuding a general atmosphere of canny benevolence, he looked like any one of a hundred thousand similar solid citizens and honest Joes who invade Europe every year.

He could have been a professor on a year's sabbatical from a mid-Western university. Or the owner of a dry-cleaning business in California who, after half an adult lifetime of reasonably honest toil, had decided to take a long vacation, a round-the-world tour. He could have been anybody—and nobody. Chamber of Commerce worthy, country club locker-room wit, Edwin Steiner was anyone's idea of the travelling American. The great international economic necessity. The human green-back, the animated dollar-bill.

To complete the camouflage, Mr Steiner was accompanied by Mrs Steiner. More accurately, he accompanied her. Mrs Steiner checked reservations, paid hotel and restaurant bills—after duly checking each item against tariff and menu. She carried about her forbidding person all the traveller's cheques, all the money. Mrs S. was suspicious of foreigners, she rode shot-gun. Her name was Effie.

Did Mr Steiner resent this apparent usurpation by his wife of his masculine prerogatives? Was he hostile to the symbol of momism he had married?

No, indeed! Between Mr and Mrs Steiner there existed in public harmony, trust, sympathy, and understanding. They stood for love—marital, international, celestial. Love to all—except, of course, the Reds. To everyone else—benevolence.

The protective colouring was complete. Edwin Steiner was a man with work to do. A dedicated man, a man with a mission. And with a slight filming of the eyes with tears she was able to turn on and off at will, Mrs S. would speak of the Great Work it was her husband's role in life to perform.

About the exact nature of this work, Mrs S. was vague. But the emotional impact of her words was generally enormous.

Her husband was Chief Executive of a U.S.-based organization to help refugees—refugees from every country, every continent . . . so she allowed it to be understood. It was the calling of this saintly man to keep in touch with refugees everywhere.

When Mrs S. was on form—and her histrionic talents were considerable—it was common for members of her audience to write out cheques to further the good work on

52

the spot. And these cheques were duly paid into a perfectly legitimate Swiss bank account.

A good performance by the couple had produced as much as fifty thousand dollars—tax deductible, of course, and mostly from fellow Americans—at a single session in some bar. Mr Steiner drinking milk.

On one memorable occasion, in the Castelana Hilton in Madrid, one homesick Yankee, after imbibing nearly a fifth of Old Grandad in patriotic enthusiasm, had subscribed a hundred thousand dollars to the cause on the spot—to the immense consternation of the floosie he was travelling with.

The money was duly paid into account.

And, it would be true to say, funds were generally used 'to keep an eye on refugees—our brothers and sisters in distress'—the phrase used by Mrs Steiner when in a fund-raising frenzy—the only deductions being to defray the legitimate, but not inconsiderable, travelling expenses of the Steiners.

But who could object to that? They lived in de luxe, hotels, but not ostentatiously. They ate the food of the country, and Edwin Steiner had never been seen to take a drink.

He did drink—but only in his hotel room late at night.

Drink was Steiner's secret vice, his lust for power the more public one. Occasionally, but then obsessively, sex troubled him—and his thoughts and desires turned to young and lithesome creatures, different indeed from Effie who was in the middle forties and turned the scale at 170 pounds.

And Mrs S.'s interests also turned in interesting directions.

On that café terrace, in Kerkira, also within sight of the Albanian coast, as Steiner watched an Italian girl, with jet-black hair and a figure of remarkable nubility, uncompromisingly revealed in a skin-tight silk dress, Mrs S. was engrossed by the performance going on in the dust at her feet.

Two urchins, evidently brothers, tumbled and rolled like

53

diminutive, perverse clowns, revelling in the dirt and the sharp stones—and in the amusement, and the horror, of the tourists who watched. They played together in a well rehearsed choreography of their own, leaping, writhing, twisting, their feet stamping to the transistorized twist of a Danish couple's radio.

Mrs S. watched, fascinated, her fork holding yet another mouthful of the delicious, sticky pastry in mid-air. The elder of the two brothers—perhaps fourteen—with a Murillo face and the sharp-featured cunning of a scavenger dog—seeing Mrs S.'s interest, rolled over and over on the flinty surface. His flesh showed through his already torn shirt. He leapt, he grovelled, he twisted like a demented snake. And soon the blood came, on his back, his legs, his arms.

When Mrs S. saw the blood, she opened her mouth and put the sweetness on her fork into it, and her happiness was complete.

Others on the café terrace cried out in pity. The poor child! Compelled to bleed, to prise with his misery a few drachmas from the tourists' pockets! A waiter tried to shoo the boys away, but they aped his words and gestures with such deadly, grotesque accuracy that the tourists clapped and the boys received the coins, tossed into the dust, that the waiter believed should have been his.

The elder of the two boys sidled up to Mrs S. and held his blood-stained arm for her to see, looking at her humbly but yet with complicity. She shivered. He was like a miniature, mercenary, sensual fakir.

She gave him fifty drachmas. Fifty!

Steiner drew his eyes away from the Italian girl and smiled indulgently. He knew what would happen.

It happened. As Mrs Steiner rose, he said, lazily, 'I think, Effie, I'll stay on here for another half-hour.'

'Suit yourself.'

'Just while you're taking your shower before dinner.' His eyes strayed back to the Italian girl. She looked at him, half smiled. It would be easy. 'No hurry,' he said. 'Take your time.' His own Italian was elementary but adequate.

'All right, Edwin.'

The boy was watching her, holding the fifty drachs, his eyes filled with dog-like devotion. Mrs S. pretended to ignore him. Steiner laughed to himself. It was ridiculous. Once, back home—when they had a home—in Baltimore they had had a dog, a dirty mongrel. He loathed that dog. Effie doted on it. She'd take it for walks, on a lead, after keeping it in suspense for minutes, with not so much as a glance in its direction, the dog suffering agonies of suspense, whimpering.

The boy whimpered now. Mrs S. let him suffer, collected her belongings—her purse, her sun-glasses, her pack of Lucky Strike, her lighter, her guide-book to the island, with maddening slowness.

'I may be a little more than half an hour,' Steiner said, watching the girl as she lazily lit a cigarette. She had been on the boat coming over from Brindisi. Now and then, beside the *Appia*'s pool, wearing a white one-piece swim-suit, depending on the light, she had looked nude.

'Maybe an hour,' he said.

'As long as you like,' Mrs S. said.

He watched her moving off across the square towards the hotel, the boy trotting at her heels, sure of himself now, out of his misery. 'Walkie-walkie,' he murmured to himself. 'Walkie-walkie!'

He saw her disappear into the hotel, passing the saluting porter to whom no doubt she had said a magic word to let the urchin pass.

Now she would be sailing up to the reception desk, sur-prisingly quick and even delicate in her movement for such a fat woman.

'My key, please. Number 37.'

The glance of the obsequious clerk would flutter over the boy, mildly disapproving, questioning.

55

'Oh, I'm taking this poor little boy up to my room. Send up a bottle of Coca-Cola.'

And she would move on to the elevator, the boy at her heels, most probably thumbing his nose—or perhaps even winking—at the attendant.

Edwin Steiner sincerely hoped his wife would amuse herself. He, too, rose and moved to the Italian girl's table.

'*Ciao!*'

The girl looked at him challengingly, her eyes passing over his Sulka tie, his crumpled but obviously silk and expensive suit, his gold wristwatch, his Jap camera, assessing the value of his personal effects to the nearest hundred lire. Or so it seemed to Steiner.

He smiled as he pulled the vacant chair towards him. '*Permette!*'

Ten minutes later, after Steiner had bought her a brandy and made it clear time wasn't on their side, they were walking together towards a seedy waterfront hotel. She said her name was Lola.

Steiner paid two hundred drachs for the room in advance. It was hot and airless, but at least clean. This he verified by turning back the sheets on the bed. Then he locked the door. He had removed his jacket and was taking off his tie when he caught sight of her in the fly-blown dressing-table mirror. She stood perfectly still, watching him, not one inch of her dress unzipped.

Steiner took five hundred drachs from his notecase, held it up for her to see, said '*Cinque cento!*'—and put the notes down within her reach on the dressing-table.

Still the girl did not move. Steiner was hot in that stuffy room, and irritated. Moving around the world so much he never had time for the finesse of sex, for women who played it coy or hard to get. He liked service fast and efficient, in return for good money, both in the restaurant and the bedroom.

56

'What now?' he demanded, his voice harsh. 'Not enough?'

'Plenty,' she said quietly. 'Thank you.'

'Then what's eating you? Get undressed.'

Still the girl did not move. Suddenly Steiner realized that he, in his irritation, had spoken, and she had replied, in English. In a flash, his instincts spelled danger, and opposition of any kind always gave him goose-flesh, produced adrenalin, the urge to lash out.

He went up close to her, grasped her chin, his fingers digging into the flesh.

'What's the matter with you? All smiles and sweet-talk out on the sidewalk. In the bedroom you clam up—except for one word *in English!*' He dug in his fingers a little harder, then let go. The print of thumb and four fingers showed angrily red on her cheeks.

In that humid room, suddenly she was trembling. Was it possible she was the contact? He dismissed the idea at once. She would have identified herself as soon as they were alone.

'How much English do you know?'

She shook her head. 'A little. . . .'

Now Steiner was convinced of one thing. He hadn't picked up Lola, she had picked him up. After hundreds of pick-ups Steiner was an expert on form. This one wasn't running to form. Why?

'Lola who?' he demanded.

'Does it matter?'

'It matters.' He caught her a stinging blow.

'Montini,' she said.

'Me?' he rasped, 'Why pick on me? I'm such a glamour-puss? I look so well-heeled? I'm fat, over forty and a bastard to women—and it probably shows. Why me?'

He took a step towards her, beginning to enjoy himself. He grabbed her by the shoulders, turned her round, found the zip and pulled. The silk dress fell to her ankles.

Lola was wearing pants and bra in scarlet. Steiner let his eye travel slowly over the smooth olive skin. She was more

57

than a little on the plump side, but he liked that—the indolent voluptuousness, he guessed, of a Sicilian.

There was nothing indolent about what happened a split second later. The girl stepped neatly out of the silk embracing her ankles. Twisting round to face him a stiletto appeared in her hand as if it were a natural extension of the limb. Sheathed in the top of her stocking, warmed by her thigh, it now pointed directly at him, six inches of flat, needle-sharp steel flicking at him like a snake's tongue.

Steiner snarled and lunged at her. The stiletto struck. Blood stained his arm. His astonishment became a cold fury. He grabbed the only weapon he had, a flimsy wooden chair, and used it like an animal trainer against a newly captured beast that had already tasted blood. He moved warily but with a kind of superiority, of contempt—man matching superior intelligence and skill against brute.

She was too quick for him. When he tried to pin her against the wall, she slipped aside. The stiletto flashed again, drawing a thin red line down his cheek.

Till that instant, he hadn't really believed she intended to kill him. Now he was certain of it. This wasn't some perverse game, but a gladiatorial combat. One of them had to die.

Steiner, ordinarily a controlled man, master of mind, nerve and muscle, began to sweat. She had kicked off her shoes, and they fought, in a grotesque parody of love-play, in an extraordinary silence, almost meeting, recoiling, avoiding, yet wishing the final, fatal union. If either of the adjoining rooms had been occupied, and if the occupants had been interested, nothing unusual would have been heard, at least for that particular shabby waterfront hotel.

The sounds of love and death can be oddly similar.

Now that the element of surprise in her attack was discounted, he knew the outcome was a matter simply of strength and reach. He was superior in both. As they circled one another Steiner smiled his pleasure. He would disarm the girl, then force her to confess the reason for the threat. For years, confessions had been Steiner's business.

Steiner feinted with the chair to the left and she moved, as he had anticipated, to the right, the direction in which his weight was already poised.

Now he lunged in earnest—and the four legs of the chair held her immobile against the whitewashed wall. The knife was neutralized, jabbing vainly at air.

Holding the chair firmly against the wall, Steiner reached forward and grabbed the girl's wrist. Then he let go of the chair and twisted the wrist behind her back.

She whimpered with pain and the knife fell to the floor. Steiner picked it up then, released her, thrust her away from him.

'Now,' he said pleasantly, 'let's have it. Your real name, who you're working for, and why you were ordered to eliminate me.'

Holding the knife directly pointing towards her chest, just as she had levelled it at him, Steiner moved towards her.

'Don't think about it,' he murmured. 'Just talk.' He pressed the needle-sharp point of the knife against her skin, not hard, just enough to draw a single drop of blood.

'Don't be shy,' he said easily as the girl gave a tiny gasp of fear and pain, 'just a little louder, that's all.'

The girl's lips were parted and dry. Her tongue moistened them as if she were about to speak. But no sound came except a swift intake of breath which summoned her last reserves of will and resolution. Then she flung herself forward to him, arms outstretched as if seeking embrace.

Steiner felt her skin against his fist. He shrank back, staring at her, horrified, incredulous.

The girl had sagged back against the wall, and for a

moment she stayed there, the knife buried in her breast up to the hilt. Then, slowly, like a puppet at the end of the show, she sagged to the floor.

Murder, planned with infinite care and executed by proxy, was Steiner's profession—the murder of men's bodies and, more often, the murder of their souls.

But this was the first time the blood of a victim had ever touched his own hands.

Steiner winced with astonishment and distaste. Why? None of it made sense. That is, if his cover was as sound as he had every reason to believe it to be. Edwin Steiner was a harmless, itinerant American, roaming the world with malice towards none. The people who had reason to fear him were so terrified, if not for themselves then for their wives and children, husbands or parents, that not one of them would dare risk revenge, reprisals.

Steiner stared at the corpse, flipping rapidly through a mental card-index. The girl fitted nowhere.

Steiner was disturbed, jumpy, but did not panic. For several seconds, he stood quite still, listening. From inside the hotel, nothing. From outside, the faint murmuring, shuffling second rebirth of the town as it emerged with the failing light from siesta. Soon the streets would be seething, a good-natured, anonymous mass of people flowing turgidly in the timeless ritual of the *passeggiata*.

Suddenly Steiner began to move, purposively, swiftly. From the breast-pocket of his jacket, he took a clean white handkerchief. Stooping over the corpse, he wiped the handle of the knife clear of finger-prints, without removing the weapon from the wound.

The chair received similar treatment, as did every other article of furniture in the room.

For a moment he considered what to do about the girl. Left where she was, the body would be discovered by some servant in a matter of perhaps minutes after his departure. Under the bed whose sheets reached to the floor, in such an unfastidious establishment, it might be a matter of hours—perhaps, with any luck, even a couple of days. The drains, the waterfront, refuse, cooking odours and a near-by butcher's shop were his accessories.

Three minutes later, perspiring from the exertion, Steiner looked around the room. Nothing was out of place, no blood on the floor, no hint of death. Instead of being an arena, again it was just an hotel room—like all hotel rooms everywhere, cheap and expensive, tasteful and sordid, impersonal, discreet, indifferent, oblivious, just so many cubic feet of space hired perhaps for love, for sleep, for suicide, for refuge, and sometimes for murder.

Cautiously, Steiner unlocked the door, eased it open. The corridor was empty. He slipped out, relocked the door, leaving the key.

The porter sat behind the desk in exactly the same attitude as forty minutes ago, reading a newspaper, a glass of beer beside him.

Without pausing, Steiner walked towards the exit. The porter did not look up—discretion being one of his principal qualifications for the job—but said, 'The key, sir?'

'Upstairs,' Steiner said, indistinctly, not stopping.

'Okay,' the porter said, his eyes not leaving the printed page. This was normal. Clients arrived together but seldom left at precisely the same time.

Steiner took a gulp of the fishy, ouzo air and then, head down, thrust his way through the slow tide of girls, couples, children, whole families that now flowed through the streets.

Take it easy, he told himself. Run, and everyone looks at you. Walk, and no one cares. Just another tourist.

Steiner took his time getting back to his own hotel.

The clerk behind the reception desk wore striped pants, a starched collar and a deferential smirk.

'Mrs Steiner *is* in, sir,' he said in his American accent—

61

he had the appropriate one for most of the tourist nationalities. 'Shall I call her?' His hand moved to the internal phone.

'Why?' Steiner demanded. 'I'm going straight up.' Of course he knew damn well why. The clerk knew all about the gipsy boy and expected to be, or already had been rewarded for sounding the alarm. He made a deprecating gesture, but Steiner was already on his way to the elevator.

He turned abruptly. 'No messages?'

The clerk glanced at the rack, though he already knew the answer. 'No messages, sir.'

Steiner took a cigar from his case and let the clerk light it for him. 'Send up anything the moment it arrives.'

'Of course, sir.'

'Or anybody.' He gave the fellow twenty-five drachs. 'And send up a bucket of ice. Now.'

'At once.' He coughed discreetly. 'And a doctor, perhaps?'

'A doctor? What the devil for?'

The clerk said nothing but let his fingers stray, significantly, to his own cheek. The gesture made Steiner aware of a burning sensation on his own face, a sticky wetness around the collar.

He took a handkerchief and pressed it to his face. It came away stained red. The clerk watched with diffident concern.

'Someone . . .' Steiner searched for the convincing lie, 'someone jumped me in an alley.'

The clerk's concern deepened. Trained in the official school of tourism he had all the right reflexes. 'Attacked, sir!' His hand reached for the phone. 'The police must be informed at once.'

'No!'

The clerk looked puzzled. 'You don't *wish* to lodge a complaint, sir?'

'Someone just forgot their manners. It happens. Forget it.'

Steiner moved to the elevator. As usual, when things went wrong, he felt unreasonably furious with his wife. If she didn't disgust him so much, physically, then he wouldn't have to go to the broads. It was, to him anyway, as simple as that. He banged violently on the door of their room, knowing it would be locked. When it didn't open in five seconds, he banged again.

'Who's there?'

He heard her irritated, don't-disturb-I'm-busy voice from behind the door.

Mrs S. was wearing a floral kimono, looked flushed, hurt and ridiculous. Also angry.

'What the hell!' she said, her face twitching with that nervous tic. 'You said an hour. Pretty, but no talent? That it?' Then she laughed. 'You look a mess! She did that to your face?'

'Shut up!' He slammed the door behind him and began peeling off his jacket. 'And get that kid out of here!'

'You live your private life, I'll live mine. Wasn't that the bargain?' She was truculent now, pleased by his discomfiture. 'Don't you think it would be nice and friendly if you just had a quick clean-up and then went quietly to the bar for a cool, soft drink?'

For a second Steiner contemplated the jeering, well hated face, then struck it.

He said again, 'Get the kid out of here!' and went to the bathroom, not once glancing towards the bed. 'And bring the whisky!'

The place reeked of soap and cologne. Evidently the ritual washing had already been performed. Steiner examined his face in the mirror. Three deep scratches from cheek-bone to chin where the girl had left her mark. He washed his face carefully, wincing with the pain, and dabbed the wounds with Dettol, applying the largest invisible plaster he could find.

As he pressed the edges of the plaster, he thought about

63

the whisky and the solace, relief and clarification of mind just one man-sized shot, well iced, would bring.

Where the hell was it? Already he had heard her taking the ice from the waiter at the door.

'Well, what's keeping you?' he shouted.

Then he heard the tinkle of ice against glass.

He turned, his mouth parched, ready for the whisky, almost ready to say a reluctant, conciliatory word. But it wasn't Effie who was holding the glass.

Smiling, obsequious, washed and perfumed, it was the urchin.

'Whisky, please,' he lisped in English. 'Just one ice-cube, the way you like it, Mr Steiner.'

Steiner stared at him, astonished. The tone, the insinuating manner, the use of his name suddenly made him bristle. First the girl, now this boy. Were they both out to get him, one way or another?

Suddenly, his nerves went taut.

He pushed past the boy into his sitting-room—when staying in hotels the Steiners always enjoyed the maximum comfort possible. After all, the Organization paid.

Effie was sitting on the sofa, intently repairing her make-up. Recently, growing fatter, wrinkle creases deepening, she had started using more powder, more rouge. Her hair was dyed a vivid copper, set into tight curls, like a metal wig. She went on with the restoration work without looking up as he entered. The boy followed, still holding the whisky, deferential, intimate like a bath-house lackey.

'I thought I told you to get rid of the kid!'

Effie shrugged and went on painting red blobs on her cheek-bones. 'He didn't want to go!'

'Didn't want to! . . .' Steiner almost shouted. Of course she was needling him. 'Why not? You paid him, didn't you?'

'He didn't want to be paid, either.'

Steiner remembered the urchin's grovelling in the dirt

only an hour ago for one or two drachs. Now he was sure something was wrong.

Effie transferred her attention from her face to touching up her nails. Steiner spun round to face the boy.

'Who are you? What do you want here?'

'My name is Socrates,' the boy said. 'You want whisky now?'

'Socrates!' Steiner said, unbelievingly. 'What kind of a name is that?'

'The bell-hop here is called Plato,' his wife said. 'One of the waiters—the one like a Greek god—is called Archimedes.'

'Well, since we're representing a cultural organization, that's very cosy,' Steiner said. 'It's warming to get so close to the classics.'

'Ancient names still very common in Greece,' the boy explained, showing all his teeth.

It occurred to Steiner that his English seemed to have progressed from tourist pidgin to advanced level. He looked closely at the boy for the first time. Perhaps he wasn't around fourteen years old. Fifteen, maybe, even a year or so more? With these eastern Mediterranean types, it was hard to say.

'Okay, Socrates, what's the pitch?'

'Pitch?' A puzzled frown creased the old-young face, then the white teeth flashed. 'Pitch! Baseball! I understand. The pitch, Mr Steiner, is—I go with you, you go with me.'

'I don't quite get that, Socrates,' Steiner said. 'Explain it to me.'

'Well, sir, I go to Albania. You come along.'

So this kid, this bit of human flotsam from the streets was the contact! The person-who-would-make-himself-known he had been expecting a whole week. Well, kids made millions in show-biz, they were the people ad-men loved, governments pandered to. Youth in business, government, the arts. Why not in espionage, too!

Chinese intelligence was more with it than he had supposed.

'Okay, Soc!' Steiner said in his best scoutmaster voice. 'So you're in charge. Youth at the helm. I like that! You lead, we tag along.'

'Isn't that nice!' Effie said happily from the sofa.

Chapter Eight

Anna came round, with a vile headache, to find Sarratt sitting at the end of the bed, watching her with an expression both friendly and clinical.

He said, 'I won't ask you how you feel. I know. The M.O. could give you something to pep you up, but personally I think you've had enough drugs for a while.'

Anna stretched out an arm and discovered she was wearing a nightdress that was not her own, with a coarse institutional look and feel. Then she looked around the room and tried to remember where she was. No one's flat that she could think of. A hotel? Well, hardly. The door had no handle on the inside. Jail, again? The bed was too comfortable.

Her brain seemed to be floating in a huge black cloud. Every now and then half-formed thoughts, images, memories appeared, but vanished again before she could grasp them. Her mouth felt abominably dry, and a great lassitude possessed her. She just couldn't be bothered to ask the obvious questions. Suddenly it occurred to her that if she looked anything like she felt, she must be a sight.

She moistened her lips. 'Could I have a mirror, d'you think? And a glass of water?'

'I'll try and organize a mirror,' Sarratt said. He smiled briefly. 'But don't worry about how you look. You look fine —everything considered. As for the water—I've a better idea.'

He got up, went to the door, rapped once.

The door opened and Sarratt said something to someone she couldn't see.

He said to Anna, 'We generally keep some on ice—against emergencies. Don't bother to ask questions. I'll explain everything you want to know.' He took his cigarette case. 'Would my smoking bother you?'

'At the moment,' she said, 'nothing bothers me. But you shouldn't smoke cigarettes. You *do* read the newspapers?'

'That's what my wife used to say.'

'You don't listen to her?'

'Not any more.' He lit a cigarette, inhaled deeply. 'She's dead.'

There was a tap on the door. A moment later, Sarratt was uncorking a bottle of champagne. He said, 'It's non-vintage, I'm afraid. The powers-that-be are a little mean when it comes to the niceties. Still, I don't think that will worry you, the way you feel.'

'You seem very sure of the way I feel,' Anna said, watching him fill two glasses. 'It gives you an unfair advantage.'

'Well, we have a considerable amount of experience. From previous cases. The usual practice is to subject you to yet another examination—physical and psychological— when you come to. I dissuaded them. Meaning myself.'

'Thank you,' she said, without the slightest idea what he was talking about. She took a sip of champagne. It was too cold for the flavour to emerge. But wonderful.

As she took a second sip, quite suddenly she remembered the call from Max Giltin, Target Films, the ride down the M2.

She said, 'I didn't realize you were in the movie business, Mr Sarratt. Was the screen test a success?'

68

'Almost unqualified. Unfortunately, I can't let you see the rushes. It's against company policy.'

'Anyway, I've got the part?'

'If you want it—provided you understand just what acceptance entails.'

'Suppose you tell me, in words simple enough for a poor lost girl to understand.' She held out her glass for more champagne.

Filling it up, he said. 'Evidently you like to drink.'

'I like this drink—now. It depends—on how I feel, who I'm with. Right now I feel like drinking, and I like being with you.' She snuggled down into the bedclothes, half-smiling at him, feeling suddenly, unaccountably happy, and thinking he was the most attractive man in the forty to fifty bracket she had yet encountered.

'Of course, habitual or compulsive drinking is something we're very careful about when casting. We generally run special tests—from the ordeal of the country-house week-end, to rather underhand ones like depressing the subject by post-hypnotic suggestion and locking him or her up with a bottle.' He took a sip from his own glass. 'Such tests apply to subjects who haven't been under intensive scrutiny for some time—naturally.'

'Naturally!'

'In your case, we have a very complete dossier—covering eight months. I'm afraid you *do* like to drink—on social and sexual occasions. To intensify experience—pleasure.'

She said, 'When you're talking about intensifying things, don't exaggerate. I don't think good talk flourishes in an alcoholic fog, and I never yet heard of a man—or woman—who performed better in bed when loaded—if you'll forgive the crudity.'

'In this place,' he said, 'we forgive everything. There is no sin we are unaware of, no eccentricity unrecorded.'

'Now you're really talking like a movie-man. You'll never get a certificate for your feature.'

69

'In this place,' he said, 'we don't need certificates. Within the limits of a fairly generous budget, we're responsible to no one but ourselves.'

'So much for the build-up,' Anna said. 'Now suppose you tell me about "this place". You make it sound like a nightmare version of a psychiatrist's consulting-room and a Roman Catholic confessional.'

He smiled. 'A very fair description—except that we make sure of getting to know the truth. Here we've no time to waste on lies, self-deception, self-dramatization.'

'Very moral. Very praiseworthy.'

'Perhaps you won't think so when you hear the whole story.'

He took another cigarette and lit it slowly. 'Now, Miss Zordan, it is my duty to warn you that everything you are about to hear is covered by the Official Secrets Act. Any breach of confidence on your part could lead to a very long term of imprisonment at the very least.'

'And at most?'

'If the betrayal were serious enough, summary execution —without even the right of trial in a court of law.'

'In one of Her Majesty's prisons? By the public hangman?'

'No. Wherever you happened to be—or to have fled to. By whatever means necessary. Gun, rope, poison, apparent accident. We can be very inventive, very ingenious.'

Their eyes met and held for several seconds. His grey, hers blue. Neither flinched. Anna said, 'You're inviting me to become a spy, a secret agent?'

'Yes.' And after a pause, 'I've said we'd ruthlessly eliminate you for any betrayal. Equally, if you were caught by the other side we would disown you—unless we could do something without implicating ourselves. A good agent is valuable, but in the last resort, always expendable. You realize that?'

'Yes.' Her eyes were suddenly misty. 'That's why you never did anything about my father and mother?'

70

He nodded. 'I'm sorry. But there it is. Compared with the world of espionage, the jungle is a sweet and gentle place.'

He took a pen and a document from his pocket. He said, 'It was because of your parents in the first place that I thought you might be especially suitable for this work. Since then, events have practically thrust you into our arms.'

'That's nice!' Anna took another sip of champagne.

'I'm talking about your involvement—however remotely —with the assassination of H'an Yang. The jail sentence. That shook us at first—until we realized your somewhat beatnik motives were genuine. But after your much more intimate involvement in the death of Hagmann—H'an Yang's assassin. . . .'

'Hagmann killed him?' Anna was astonished.

'The same gun. The gun *you* used to kill Hagmann. After that, it wasn't so much a matter of inviting you to join the service but conscripting you. You were so deeply involved in the game that we just couldn't let you go.' He held out the pen and the document.

'Suppose I say no?'

'Well, we couldn't just let you run around—knowing what you know. Frankly, we'd be in an awkward position. We could bring you to trial for murdering Hagmann. You picked him up, brought him to your flat. There was a quarrel, a struggle, the gun went off. An unfortunate visitor to Britain becomes involved with an unscrupulous, vicious little tart. . . . But on the whole, we prefer quicker, less public methods.'

'Like me being found in an alley with my throat cut?'

'Something of the sort. The dead don't give evidence at an inquest.' He took another glass of the champagne himself.

'You'd better send for another bottle,' Anna told him.

'All right.' He got up and moved to the door. 'Are you hungry?'

'M'um. Now you mention it.'

'Well, we run a twenty-four-hour service in this place, though after midnight it's usually something uninteresting like steaks. That's one thing we haven't been able to beat: the reluctance of the English chef to put his heart and soul into the creation of a really delicious meal at four a.m. Although, in point of fact, the chef here at the moment is a Frenchman. Demoralized. And resting.'

'From what?'

'A particularly dangerous and uncomfortable assignment in Cambodia. One of our best agents. He adores to cook. It's therapeutic.'

Anna said, 'All right, darling. A steak—tournedos. And a French salad.'

'Garlic?'

'I adore garlic.' Anna suddenly felt tremendously gay. 'What about you?'

'I'm not eating.'

'Then neither am I.'

'Don't be childish.'

'I am not being childish, I'm being womanish.'

Sarratt threw up his hands in mock despair and rapped again on the door. It opened at once, just a few inches. He gave the order to the unseen attendant—two steaks, more champagne.

He said, 'What d'you think about food generally? I mean, being of partly Hungarian parentage, are you mad about Hungarian cooking?'

'To the exclusion of all others?'

'Yes.'

'Then the answer's "no". I eat Hungarian when I'm in an Hungarian mood.'

'Is that often?'

'Rather seldom. Don't forget I've never actually *lived* in Hungary. I'm not passionately, professionally Hungarian. I don't make a way of life, a career, out of it. You know what I mean?'

Sarratt nodded. 'I do, indeed. You're not a member of the international secret society of expatriate Magyars, with its own language, its own rites and customs, and usually a great reluctance to eat anything else but *pörkölt*, *gulyás*, chicken paprika, *rétes*, and, at Christmas, *beigli?*'

'You pronounce all that rather well,' Anna said. 'You wouldn't be a member of the society yourself, by any chance? You don't have a Hungarian fairy godmother?'

'Unfortunately no.'

'"Unfortunately"?'

'A little Hungarian in one's make-up is interesting. Just a soupçon. Like garlic in Mediterranean food.'

'I think you're interesting even without it,' Anna said. 'Anyway, how did you acquire the specialized knowledge?'

'With the British Military Mission in Hungary after the war. Since ... well, let's say that acquiring specialized knowledge of various international secret societies has been my business.'

Anna looked at him with cool appraisal, considering she had already consumed the greater part of a bottle of champagne. 'In spite of this paprika sauce, you're still very English.'

'Is that bad?'

'Well, it could be inconvenient, even dangerous, if you're a spy in a spot.'

Sarratt sighed. 'Ah, but you see, I seldom am in a spot—meaning at risk to life and limb—not in my particular field. Difficulties with subordinates, tiresome interference from politicians, wrangles over policy—all that, yes. But the kind of danger when the creak on the floorboards, the knock on the door, the chance request for a light can mean sudden death? It's not part of my world. I assess, evaluate information—as cold-bloodedly as I can. How that information is acquired, at what risk in terms of blood, nerves, sinew, is, and should be, unimportant. I'm really a sort of human computer. The agents feed the information in—and, theoretically, the right answer comes out.'

73

He looked momentarily sad, pensive. Anna said, 'And of course you'd rather be "on active service" than cooped up here or in some dingy office in Whitehall!'

He nodded. 'The leg.'

'One day you must tell me how it happened.'

Sarratt took in a loaded tray and a second bottle. Again Anna did not catch sight of the attendant.

Sarratt removed the covers from the dishes and sniffed. 'The merest soupçon!'

The steaks were large, thick, succulent. Anna's mouth watered.

Sarrett said, 'I think you'd enjoy the meal more if you signed first.' He held out the paper.

'You know, this could be very cosy,' Anna told him, 'if you didn't have such a one-track mind. Don't you ever relax?'

'Not when I've work on hand.'

'That's all I am to you? Work?'

'Pleasant work,' he conceded.

'Well, that's nice! Positively poetic!' Anna looked at the tray. 'I do hate cold food. All right, I'll sign.'

'Good.' He unscrewed the cap of his fountain pen.

'On one condition!'

'Don't be tiresome. Oh, all right. What is it?'

Anna looked at him challengingly, her lips still wet with champagne. 'Kiss me.'

After a second's pause, he said in a slightly strained voice, 'I'm sorry, Anna. For an ex-jailbird, murderess and potential spy, you're a very nice girl. But that sort of thing is expressly against company rules.'

'You mean the boss becoming emotionally involved with the female members of staff?'

'Yes.'

'That's an odd rule,' she said. 'From what I've gathered so far about this place, I should have thought it's a case of "anything goes", "expediency first", "any means justify the end", and all that jazz. You surprise me, Mr Sarratt.'

He said, 'Don't play games, Anna. Not games you'd regret.'

'I regret very little I've done in my young life,' Anna told him. 'And anyway, don't be so damned paternal—even if you are old enough. What a production about a simple kiss!'

Suddenly, it occurred to him that he was being absurd. He put down the document and the pen, and sat close to her on the edge of the bed. Their lips met.

The kiss, as it turned out, was not simple. In Hollywood, censor-wise, kisses are timed. This one went well over the limit. Her mouth was fragrant, her tongue inventive. Her bare arms entwined about his neck, holding him fiercely to her. He had almost to fight her to make her let go. Flushed, panting, triumphant, she looked up at him from the pillow. The blue eyes challenged him to make the next, obvious move.

Sarratt made a move, not instinctive, but logical, according to his point of view. He picked up the document and the pen and handed them to her. His finger pointed to the dotted line. 'Now sign,' he said.

Anna scribbled her signature without giving the document a second glance.

Sarratt took the covers off the dishes again and served the food. He opened the second bottle, refilled their glasses. For several minutes they ate in silence.

Then Anna said suddenly, '*This, drágám,* is almost like being married!' She gave a little mock whimper of distress. 'We've nothing to say any more? After everything was going so fine?'

Sarratt said, 'Well, in an odd sort of way, I'm relieved.'

'That *is* odd! Personally I'm not relieved at all.'

'One of the experts who investigated you thought you had Lesbian tendencies.'

'I'm suspicious of experts,' Anna said. 'Their terms of reference are too narrow.'

'I agree. Still, they do have their uses.' He finished his

steak and started the salad. 'I can think of occasions when a female agent with tastes of that kind might be distinctly useful.'

'In making contact with similarly disposed diplomats on the other side?'

'Exactly. Women are becoming more and more versatile. We must move with the times.'

Anna said, 'Of course I've heard how the Russians try to recruit agents among Western diplomats by compromising them on account of off-beat tendencies, but do you think that sort of thing is really "us"? The British? Not really cricket.' She finished the last morsel of steak. 'A wonderful meal,' she said. 'On second thoughts, you'd better give me that document back. To tear up!'

'Nothing doing!' Sarratt said.

'I'd do almost anything for Britain, but seducing Russian women is out.'

Sarratt smiled. 'Well, most of those I've seen around aren't particularly seductive. Anyway, I don't think you'd be much good at it. And what I say goes.'

'Thanks.'

'Save them. You'll find yourself in other spots attributable to my orders. And you'll damn me to hell.'

'That's debatable.'

'And postponable. Let's get down to here and now. Cases.'

'Yes, let's!' Anna wiggled one shoulder, wishing she were wearing the kind of nightie that slipped.

'And stop being coy,' Sarratt told her. 'I shouldn't have ordered that second bottle of champagne.'

'Rubbish! And don't underestimate my susceptibility to alcohol. My mind's perfectly clear and lucid, my speech unslurred. I imagine alcohol is one of a spy's most serious hazards. And I am undergoing a whole series of alcoholic and non-alcoholic tests to see how I measure up.' Anna held out her glass. 'Okay. Test me some more.'

Sarratt refilled the glass.

'Now listen carefully, Miss Zordan. Listen to what you've got into. And remember the Official Secrets document you've just signed.' He lit a cigarette. 'Not so long ago, the last government had a serious security problem. Criticism at home, criticism abroad—from our Allies in general, the U.S. in particular. Vassal, Kirby, Brown, Burgess, Maclean, Fuchs, and the rest. I don't have to go into details. Anyway the word went out from Number 10 to tighten things up. Better still, think things out afresh, from first principles. A memo, suitably coded, of course, went into an out tray. . . .'

'And reached you.'

Sarratt nodded. 'For some time I'd had a fairly close connexion with M.I.5, the Special Branch of Scotland Yard, and various other security and intelligence outfits—as a sort of co-ordinator. I was a kind of one-man department, with a nice title, a certain status, but absolutely no power. I made recommendations everyone ignored.'

'Then the Prime Minister waved his magic wand?'

'My brief was quite simple, and extremely secret. "Set up a new security and intelligence organization. An organization that will exist side-by-side with, independently of, and unknown to every other intelligence organization in the country. You will have almost unlimited powers, adequate finance, complete freedom to operate in any way you think fit".' He looked at her quizzically. 'That meant hiring anyone I thought suitable.'

'And amongst others, you thought of me?' Anna paused. 'So, after my encounter with Hagmann, I can count myself very fortunate I phoned you, not the police?'

Sarratt nodded. 'As an old aunt of mine used to say when things went right. It was "guidance". I can operate only as long as there's no publicity, no Fleet Street gossip, no questions in the House, no soul-searching, even at Scotland Yard. I walk a tight wire.'

77

'So here we are,' Anna said.

'In a run-down old mansion with pre-fabricated annexes "somewhere in Kent", masquerading as a film company. A polyglot collection of misfits from a score of countries who have, if I'm not mistaken, a conviction that the true champions of democracy must go underground.' He looked at her quizzically. 'Are you with me?'

'With my background, how could I not be? Body and soul.' There was a silence. Without realizing it, she began to hum a melody. It could easily have been the champagne. Equally easily, it could not.

Listening, Sarratt said, *'Sag' mir wo die Blumen sind* . . . *wann will man je verstehn.* . . .'

Anna said, 'When indeed? The catacombs?'

'I don't follow.'

'Like the early Christians. Is that us?'

'If possible, no lions. Anyway, morally, we don't measure up.'

Sarratt offered the bottle, but she waved it away. This was it. The crest of the alcoholic wave. She knew it, from experience. Intellectually, emotionally, the moment of truth.

She raised her empty glass. 'No lions!'

Silently, he too raised his glass and finished his drink.

Anna said, 'Of course you know what Cleopatra said about lame men?'

'Fact or fiction?'

'Fiction, I imagine. But true, I'm told, none the less.'

'Then tell me.'

'She said, "Lame men copulate best".'

'A crude word.'

'For, in my case, a far from crude feeling. In any case, a feeling related to you.'

Sarratt said, 'The tests indicate that you are over-sexed.'

'A nympho?'

'Not exactly, but endowed above normal.' He lit a cigarette quickly, to conceal the fact that his hand was shaking.

78

'What's normal?'

Sarratt shrugged. 'The above normal that's useful to us. In the line of duty you'll find it necessary, perhaps enjoyable.'

'So you're hiring a kind of tart?'

'Let's say we're hiring a woman with exceptional qualifications all round.'

'Okay,' Anna said. 'That straightens us out. No emotional involvement. You're probably right.'

'I'm sure I am.'

'Well, now that's out of the way, what next? Special training?'

'A crash course. Weapons, disguise, codes, communications. The usual things, some of them disgusting. In a war, enemies generally end up by imitating each other's methods. That's what's happening now with us. Our job is to eliminate, if possible, or at least neutralize a Chinese organization very similar to our own. To put a stop to their little drama on a world-wide scale of assassination in three acts.'

'That's what you learnt from the tape?'

Sarratt nodded, got up. Anna saw his face had suddenly become set, the lines deeply etched. A tired, moist, three a.m. face, mouth compressed, tense.

'You're unhappy suddenly?' she asked.

He didn't seem to hear her. At the door, he said, 'Oh, by the way, there's a sort of passing-out test at the end of the week—just to decide in what kind of situations you could be usefully, and reliably, employed.'

'Oral or written?'

He ignored the second question, answered the first. 'Not suddenly unhappy.' he said. 'I'm an unhappy man.' He rapped on the door which was opened at once. 'Go to sleep while you're still high.'

Chapter Nine

Even when the light's bad, which isn't often in that part of the world, you can see Albania from the coast of Corfu. Flat, swampy lowlands that give little hint of the mountain fastnesses beyond.

Though the channel is only a few kilometres wide, it was enough to scare Mrs S., who had a horror of small boats. This one in particular, smelling of oil, fish, the sweat of the two-man crew. She dabbed herself again with Molyneux Cinq.

It was cold on the water. In the darkness she drew Socrates towards her, enveloping him in mink. The feel of those bony limbs against her ample bosom. Delicious! He was so docile, so charming, so childish, yet so sophisticated. Albania, she was sure, was going to be a high-point of this trip.

The boat was running parallel with the Albanian shore now, well inside territorial waters. No lights were visible, the vessel carried no lamps of her own. Steiner, seated forward, had not uttered a word since they had left Corfu, slipping out of the harbour like just another fishing party.

The dead girl's eyes seemed to stare at him through the

blackness, but now he wasn't apprehensive of what lay behind in that hotel room, but what lay ahead. Now, Albania was a solid fact to starboard.

Five years' work, dealing with shadowy contacts, elusive as ghosts. Five years of orders, directives delivered at second and third hand. Years of conjecture, supposition, guesswork about the big boss, the brain.

Now at last the hidden fact would be revealed.

One of the two silent crew members took a torch and began flashing signals towards the coast, now a mere quarter-mile away. A distant pinpoint of light answered briefly.

Steiner went through his activities with the Organization for the tenth time since the short voyage had begun. The coup in Argentine, a free-lance affair, with rich results which he had the forethought to offer to the Chinese. The subsequent setting up of the network, first in the United States, then in Europe. Brilliant achievements, perfectly masked. Of course mistakes had been made. Inevitably.

The biggest mistake had been not to get wise to Zordan earlier. But once he had realized that the ex-Hungarian diplomat had infiltrated the Organization as a double-agent, he had had him eliminated at once, ruthlessly.

Surely, this was a matter for praise, not blame. Espionage was not an exact science. The big brain must be aware of this. The same considerations applied in the case of Briantanu. The Rumanian had seemed the perfect agent—self-effacing, confidence-inspiring. Meticulous, exact in collecting information, apparently devoted to the cause, not greedy for praise or money. Yet, suddenly, his nerve had gone.

Again, using Hagmann as the instrument of destruction, Steiner had acted at once—before Briantanu had time or opportunity to talk under drugs, hypnotism or analysis. The 'cure' had been swift, final.

81

Steiner searched his soul as if he were about to meet his maker, not a big wheel in Chinese intelligence. Hand on his heart, he did not find himself wanting.

Why then, was he so jumpy? The dead girl still stared at him.

The vessel turned now hard to starboard, straight for land, gave one lurch in the oily sea, like an ungainly seal hoisting itself ashore. The sea tried to tug it back to itself, but strong, almost invisible hands, grabbed it, heaved it farther up the beach.

Steiner winced as the muzzle of an automatic weapon was jabbed uncompromisingly into his chest. He opened his mouth. But no words of protest came. Seconds later he was being half pulled, half carried up the beach. Somewhere behind him he heard Effie protesting.

The sound stopped abruptly, in a nervous giggle.

As far as Steiner could tell, the reception committee consisted of ten, perhaps fifteen men, wearing some kind of uniform.

The man clearly leading the operation, cool, precise, methodical, was undoubtedly Chinese. He gave orders by brief gesture, force of personality, rather than by word of mouth.

Steiner fumed with irritation. He had expected a friendlier reception. When he started to light a cigarette, a guard knocked it out of his hands.

The Chinese officer saluted stiffly. 'You will both follow me.'

Steiner and his lady stumbled up the beach, then pressed blindly through a patch of scrub and stagnant water above the high-water line. Mosquitoes buzzed and zoomed viciously to the attack, attracted by sweating bodies.

Mrs S. broke the heel of a shoe, ran her stockings, lost her temper.

'Why the hell can't we have a light?' she expostulated. 'We're on dry land now, ashore in what's supposed to be a friendly country. And I'm not going a step farther until you get someone to carry my bag.'

The Chinese officer stopped, turned to face her. He said very quietly, very distinctly, 'If you speak once again you will be gagged.'

'Well, how d'you like that!' Mrs S. shrilled. 'No one speaks to Effie Steiner like that. No one! And that includes any lousy . . .'

At a gesture from the Chinese officer, a man had her arms behind her back and handcuffed. The same instant, a large piece of sticking plaster went over her mouth.

Mrs S., eyes bulging, stared from the Chinese to her husband with all the blank, stupefied incredulity of an animal trussed for slaughter.

Steiner laughed silently in her face. At last something had been done to Effie he'd been wanting to do for fifteen years.

The officer was not interested in Mrs S. any more. He stood motionless, listening intently. Then he took a heavy Luger from his belt.

Cupping his mouth, he said inaudibly into Steiner's ear, 'Now you will follow quickly. In silence. Or you also will be gagged.'

He gestured to a soldier, who unslung his automatic weapon and moved forward through the swampy scrub. Within seconds he had faded into the darkness.

Now Socrates led the little party, moving delicately, soundlessly, on bare feet. Steiner wondered how many other visitors to Albania he had guided before. The route was evidently well-planned. He plodded on, gasping, sweating, now carrying his wife's suitcase as well as his own.

The ground remained broken and swampy. Mosquitoes attacked incessantly. Always Steiner was uncomfortably aware of the Chinese moving silently behind him.

Why the need for silence? What was the danger?

Seconds later, he had a partial answer.

From somewhere ahead in the darkness came a low, gasping sob, a cry that could have been animal or human. A single, agonized, exhalation. Then silence.

Steiner froze in his tracks. His wife's tongue fought against the gag. Socrates stopped, the perpetual smile for once extinguished.

A soldier, crouching, moved forward, gun out-thrust, in the direction of the cry. Steiner sensed rather than heard rapid, retreating footsteps over to the right. Mrs S. wondered whether to play the helpless woman, flop down on the wet earth, refuse to go on. She decided against it, encouraged by a jab with the Luger.

After twenty yards they came upon the advance patrol, lying with his face in a pool of stagnant water on top of his automatic rifle, both hands grasped firmly round stock and barrel, very dead.

The officer turned him over on his back. His ragged tunic was pierced by a single hole where a dagger had driven to the heart with deadly precision.

Quickly, the officer forced the dead fingers to give up the gun, then stood staring into the darkness through which—how many miles away—was the Greek frontier. Steiner saw his lips drawn back, exposing his teeth, in a wordless grin of rage, grimacing at a faceless enemy.

The Chinese pulled the trigger. Bullets ripped out across the swamp, shattering the huge silence.

Socrates pushed Mrs S. into an ungainly gallop. Steiner followed.

Five minutes later, the ground levelled out. They were upon the helicopter almost before they realized it. Black, silent, the perspex of its cockpit glinting, eye-like in the faint light, it loomed over them, like a giant spider.

Figures closed in on them from nowhere. More Chinese. One said, in English, 'Inside, please!' A light-weight ladder appeared at the side of the machine.

The automatic rifle fire of their escort had stopped. But

the new bunch of Chinese seemed oblivious. All heavily armed, evidently their job was to guard the helicopter. Nothing else. The others were expendable.

Gasping, her hands released, Mrs S. made the cabin.

The motor came to life and Steiner removed the plaster from his wife's mouth. She looked around wildly as the machine, with a slight jerk, took to the air.

'Where's the boy? she demanded shrilly. 'Where's Socrates?'

The observer turned, shrugged his incomprehension, grinned. He, also, was Chinese.

'Not coming with us!' Steiner shouted, and laughed as his wife burst into tears.

The helicopter flew at about five thousand feet, Steiner figured. Above sea-level. Subtract two or three thousand if you counted the tops of the successive ranges they were flying over.

The pilot handled the machine with almost insolent skill, oblivious to the turbulence that now and then hit the tiny craft, flying in radio silence, but, judging from the dawn glow, in a north-north-easterly direction. As the light strengthened, the ruggedness of the country became more and more apparent. Mountains unfolded in an immense relief-map below. The valleys seemed almost totally enclosed by great walls of rock. Here whole armies could be swallowed up in the vastness without trace.

A country of isolated, tribal communities, Steiner remembered reading somewhere, each a law unto itself. A country of blood-feuds and vendettas, which, through the centuries, had been a headache to Turks, Slavs, Greeks, Italians. An uncomfortable dependency—a prickly ball tossed about in the blood-sport of Balkan politics for centuries. A country that had filled many strange roles in history—and now was filling the strangest of all. An outpost of Red China in the West.

Did the Chinese overlords, Steiner wondered, live as precariously in this wild land, as the other occupiers before them?

As the rocks below turned from grey to brown, then, dramatically, to red, as if the heat came from within the earth instead of from the rising sun, the helicopter began to lose height.

Mrs S. had long since subsided into silence, unable to compete with the roar of the engine. Cramped and comfortless, she had relapsed into the apathy of a first-class passenger who, by the unaccountable incompetence of a travel agency, finds herself trapped in steerage.

Now she was ready to erupt again in terror as the helicopter's rate of descent increased. Down as fast as an express lift. Within seconds they were looking up at the peaks, not down, roaring within inches, it seemed, of sheer mountain wall, hurtling along a box canyon to what seemed like certain destruction, only to leap over the crags at the end with split seconds to spare.

Mrs S. screamed. The navigator turned and grinned, as if the crew had been complimented for some exceptional display of aeronautical skill.

Five hundred feet below, an extraordinary sight was suddenly revealed.

After the barren mountains, a lush, green valley, threaded by a silver stream, with fat cattle grazing peacefully, until put to brief flight by the noise of the machine. The floor of the valley itself was not more than a few hundred yards wide at most, but cultivation in steps continued up the sides, making use of every inch of usable soil.

To Steiner the scene seemed infinitely strange, yet oddly familiar, like a picture in some book remembered from childhood.

He frowned in the effort of recall. Then he had it.

It was as if he had been transported to China. Not the China of teeming cities, of industrial masses labouring to

86

fulfil the latest plan, of parades in honour of the triumph of the Revolution.

This was the China, timeless, immemorial, of peasants and warlords, the China that missionaries know.

The helicopter zoomed a little up one side of the enclosing mountain. And there, suddenly, as if to confirm what his imagination had already told him, built into solid rock, was the warlord's fastness, white-painted, flower-encrusted, oddly sybaritic, like a millionaire's hide-away, or some very special hotel. Steiner noted more utilitarian buildings, like barracks, down in the valley.

With the delicacy of a wasp settling on a lump of sugar, the helicopter landed on a flat piece of land no bigger than a tennis court.

As the engine died, Mrs S. noticed a captive tennis ball slung between two poles, and began to relax, thinking the scene wasn't too unlike someone's dream-place back home.

Then she saw something else hanging, and swinging a little, in the dawn breeze.

The body of a man, his hands secured behind him, just as hers had been, hanging from a post used, surely, for basket-ball.

Instead of saying something pleasant to Steiner for a change, Mrs S. screamed. An emotional arrival.

Chapter Ten

Over the next few days, Anna learned the techniques of the job, methods of self-preservation, similar in many respects for both criminal and spy. She discovered how to use, and how to detect, hidden miniature microphones and transmitters, explosives and booby-traps. She practised lip-reading in five languages, how to kill a man or woman silently, with a knife. How to escape from jail—this last from a small, foxy man who did not identify himself, except to say he had escaped from various awkward situations himself, several times. One of her teeth was drilled to accommodate the tiny regulation lethal pill.

The instruction was individual. Anna saw no one but her teachers. Of other pupils there was no sign, except for the long corridor with closed, handleless doors. Work went on, with brief respites, from eight a.m. till midnight and after. Meals she took solitary in her room. There was no radio, no TV, books, newspapers or magazines, nothing to divert her from the essential task of absorbing unfamiliar knowledge. A doctor examined her several times, especially after strenuous exercise in armed, and unarmed, combat sessions.

One night, after one a.m. as she was climbing into

bed exhausted, Sarratt came in, without knocking. Anna had become used to unheralded intrusions at all hours of the day and night which were, no doubt, all part of the process of conditioning her to be always vigilant, always ready to snap awake and start thinking, acting without hesitation.

Sarratt glanced at her briefly, but offered no greeting or personal comment. His voice cold, clipped, he came straight to the point.

'About Hagmann's luggage which was found at the K.L.M. Terminal. A single suitcase. It contained some interesting literature. As well as being a "businessman" he was evidently connected with a politico-cultural outfit. Virulently anti-Communist. On the surface. Of course it's been checked by British and U.S. security agencies. And cleared. Its literature is full of such phrases as "The writers and intellectuals of Europe, the Middle East, Asia, the whole world must unite to fight Communism. There can be no co-existence with the ultimate evil ...!" It's run by an American called Steiner. You know the kind of thing?'

'Calculated to appeal to the more hysterical elements in the U.S.?'

Sarratt nodded. 'And drawing substantial contributions —tax-deductible, of course—from firms and individuals anxious to promote cheque-book warfare, the battle to be kept as far from Uncle Sam's shores as possible.'

'Don't be cynical about America,' Anna said. 'My mother was American.'

'I knew her. Once she said, after a couple of drinks, "Do you think the Foundling Fathers and Abe Lincoln would be satisfied with the state of the nation as it is today"?'

'Mother was an idealist,' Anna said. 'Let's get back to the Steiner organization.'

'Steiner,' Sarratt said. 'Edwin Steiner. The Chief Executive. He has an office in Washington, D.C. Another in Frankfurt, Germany. Actually, he spends most of his time

89

travelling, contacting intellectuals everywhere, winning them over.'

'By persuasion?'

'Partly. But his chief methods are money, favors, inviting them to meetings in pleasant places—all expenses paid, naturally. Of course most of them sing suitable songs for their supper. It seems harmless enough.'

'*If* intellectuals selling their independence for a mess of pottage can ever be considered harmless.'

'The latter-day treason of the clerks?' Sarratt shrugged. 'Perhaps. The point is, many of Steiner's contacts among the so-called intellectuals are also scientists, technicians, engineers who hold important jobs in industry and scheduled work.'

'But, as far as the British and U.S. intelligence are concerned, Steiner is a nice guy?'

Sarratt nodded. 'Buying up the right sort of people with non-government funds and saving the American tax-payer money.'

Anna said, 'What made you suspicious of Steiner? You and nobody else?'

'I don't really know. Perhaps he was so completely the all-American do-gooder to be true. Anyway I had him watched. Early last month, Paris and Brussels. Then a few days each in Lisbon, Madrid, Barcelona. The same pattern in each city. He meets several East European exiles. Cosy cultural exchanges, innocent no doubt in many cases. But a Czech he contacted in Madrid *is* working on hush-hush U.S. naval installations in Cadiz. A Hungarian he met in Paris, said to be a considerable poet in his own language, is also a nuclear scientist working on the French bomb. And in Brussels he met a Pole who used to play the fiddle in the Warsaw Philharmonic and is now a very much in-the-know economics statistician at the headquarters of the Six.'

'That doesn't prove they're spies.'

'No. But the Czech does have a Swiss bank account, the Hungarian has a stake in a chain of American laundromats, and the Pole bought many gold pieces the day after Steiner left. He also bought his wife a ring—diamond solitaire—for a hundred thousand Belgian francs.'

'She must be pretty!'

'On the contrary. But obviously a sound investment.'

'There's a lot to be said for marriage,' Anna said. 'Is Steiner married?'

Sarratt cocked an eye at her. 'In a weird sort of way.'

'A witch? Or have I got the consonant wrong?'

'According to Adler, there isn't a lot of difference. Anyway, she's ugly as sin, goes with him everywhere on all his travels, and fancies small boys. And not, apparently, because she was never a mother.'

'Fascinating woman!'

'She plays the role of secretary and general manager of the Organization, attends most of the meetings, makes reservations, pays bills, holds the cash—like many American women—and plays nurse to Steiner.'

'He's sick?'

'Well, in a vague sort of way. A martyr to the sacred cow of international understanding. I suppose it's good for the image of the movement. And of course it's more difficult to suspect a sick man of double-dealing.'

'You've seen his medical records?'

'No. But our men in both Brussels and Barcelona kept an eye on his hotel after he was supposed to have retired for the night. In the small hours, he visited brothels in both cities, where, according to our information, he acquitted himself in a way remarkable, not to say, foolhardy, for a man in his condition.'

Sarratt lit another cigarette and watched her quizzically, his expression carefully composed, detached. He said, 'Steiner's putting on weight, but he moves quickly when he has to, like a well-fed tom. He looks benevolent, easy-going, even sleepy, but he's a first-class organizer, a sharp brain, and, I'd say, utterly ruthless.'

'A warning?'

'He's your pigeon, provided you pass the final test. I want to know who he's really working for, where the HQ is, facts about his Chinese bosses.'

Anna said, 'Chinese bosses? Then why was H'an Yang murdered? It doesn't make sense.'

'Not to you and me perhaps. But to a dedicated Chinese Communist? Suppose there are two factions in Peking. The war-is-inevitable-with-the-non-Communist-world group. And the more moderate chaps who believe in trade with the West, diplomatic lovey-dovey, and so on.'

'Men like H'an Yang?'

'Exactly. Charming, cultured, skilled negotiators, guardedly pro-Western. Isn't it possible he was liquidated to discourage the others—those with similar ideas in Peking?' Sarratt paused, lit a cigarette. 'And not just in Peking, but influential men everywhere. Just suppose there was a whole series of assassinations—hundreds, perhaps thousands. Politicians, scientists, businessmen, professors, civil servants, in dozens of Western countries, without distinction of race, colour, politics—the kind of people who could be relied on to stiffen morale in a time of crisis. A deadly plague striking only at the men at the top. Effective government, particularly government favouring conciliation and peace might well come to a standstill. There would be panic, universal suspicion, probably war. And without firing a shot, or even possessing an effective bomb, the real enemy would have won.' He paused. 'That's what I gathered from the tape. But for immediate action, just three "executions".'

'So we're up against a tryout? A pilot scheme?'

Sarratt nodded. 'And we've got to use it to get at *them*—the people Steiner works for.' He crushed out his cigarette, 'It's a rotten assignment to involve you in.'

'Because I'm female?'

'Because of the things that can happen to female spies. Cruelty always seems worse when applied to a woman.'

'Your last sentimentality?'

'Perhaps. Cynical I may be. But pathologically cruel I am not. I want you to remember this. In spite of what happens.'

'I wouldn't blame you if I was ill-used abroad.'

'Not abroad. Here.'

Sarratt got up suddenly, went to the door and rapped. It opened at once. Two women, eyes unseeing, faces utterly devoid of expression, stood on the threshold. They wore white jackets, with sleeves rolled up to the elbows, grey skirts, black stockings, flat-heeled shoes.

Like nurses, Anna thought, nurses who themselves had gone mad, in some hideous asylum for the criminally insane.

Suddenly she was terrified. She shrank back against the wall, her lips parted.

Sarratt gestured towards Anna. The two women entered the room, seized her by the arms and shoulders and lifted her bodily from the bed. Anna looked at him dumbly, too terrified and astonished to speak.

As they dragged her to the door, Sarratt answered her unspoken question. He said, 'Unfortunately, all the things we have to know about a recruit can't be discovered when the subject is under drugs, hypnosis or the effects of champagne.'

When they had gone, Sarratt lit another cigarette, and waited ten minutes. What had the Nazi war criminals said? 'I am not responsible!' Well, he *was* responsible.

Responsible for selection of recruits, methods of assessment of personality including this. The T-test. T for Torture.

For weeks, when setting up the organization, he had debated with himself and a handful of specialists whether such a test was necessary.

Reluctantly he had finally decided that it was, and he

flattered himself—if that was the word—that at the end of a week he knew as much about his recruits, including their physical characteristics under stress, as the Russians or the Americans knew about their potential astronauts after months.

Till this moment, after a score of agents had passed through his hands, he had felt calmly, unemotionally convinced that the test was necessary. Torture, in many countries, would be the inevitable lot of an agent, if captured. It was vital to know how they would stand up.

Now, for the first time, he had misgivings. His hand shook as he glanced at his watch, rubbed out his cigarette.

He walked down the corridor, took the lift to the basement.

With his own pass-key he opened a door and entered what at first sight looked like a miniature producer's room in a TV studio.

Several screens were mounted over the control panel. There were loudspeakers, headphones, six independent tape-decks. A technician sat at the panel smoking a small Dutch cigar and reading a paperback novel which he put aside as Sarratt entered.

Neither spoke, nor looked at the other.

Sarratt glanced at the dials that registered the subject's pulse and respiration. Already, before commencement of the test, the readings were higher than those recorded during any previous medical examination. This was to be expected. Apprehension would produce the same effect with almost any patient in a dentist's chair. The encephalograph and sweat recorders told the same story of fear and dread.

The question was: How much could the subject stand before crying 'Enough!'

It was incredible, Sarratt reflected, how much pride entered into it . . . a kind of vanity in one's ability not to chicken out. That, probably, was what the test really added up to. A test of vanity. He knew. At first hand.

94

After making the decision to incorporate the test in the procedure, he had insisted on taking it himself—against medical advice.

So far, only one man, a Japanese—significant?—had bettered his performance.

Sarratt lit another cigarette and poured himself a cup of black coffee. He removed his jacket and loosened his tie. He nodded to the technician, who started one of the tape recorders going at three and a quarter inches per second— high fidelity not being of paramount importance—and switched on one of the screens.

Then Sarratt himself pressed a black button and a red light glowed immediately in front of him.

A gasping sound that brought beads of perspiration to his face, came from the loudspeaker.

For several seconds he could not bring himself to look at the screen.

Chapter Eleven

As a connoisseur of hospitality, measured as a test of his prestige, Steiner was partially satisfied. The hospitality he received was always generous. His hosts either expected favours, or were frankly terrified. In either case, the results were gratifying.

This, certainly, wasn't Albania as he'd imagined it.

A duplex apartment, with a refrigerator in the bedroom and a full bottle of bourbon on the table under the window which commanded a grandiose view. Tolerably efficient plumbing, comfortable furniture, orthopedic twin beds.

The jarring notes were the sentry parading up and down the terrace below, the corpse swinging from the gallows, and of course, the locked door.

Standing at the open window, Steiner wondered out loud if the corpse wasn't real—just a dummy, a gag, a gimmick.

Mrs S. didn't agree. 'It's real,' she said. 'It's a man. In this place, I'm afraid, honey!'

It was a long time since Mrs S. had called Mr S. honey in private.

Steiner frowned. In some ways he trusted her completely. About places, situations, people, she was seldom wrong.

He glanced at his watch. Four p.m.

Nearly thirteen hours since their arrival, and still not a sign of their host!

Steiner took a second shower—it was still oppressively hot in spite of the lengthening shadows—and a shot of bourbon, to soothe his nerves. He felt angry, insulted and hungry. So far they had been offered nothing more than admittedly good coffee by a voiceless Albanian servant. Who unlocked the door, who relocked it? Why was the door locked at all?

He took another drink. Mrs S., lying on her bed, painted her nails.

Suddenly he had had enough. He strode to the door and banged on it violently. Surprisingly, it opened at once. The cutest Chinese doll stood on the threshold.

Raven-black hair, olive skin, figure encased in a cheong-san of cunning cut. Steiner's irritation ebbed away as he took in every detail. The girl's eyes were downcast.

'You will follow me, please!' This demurely, palms pressed together.

'Why, certainly!'

'Aren't you the lucky one!' Mrs S. said. 'But watch yourself. You hear!'

Apart from a large, life-size statue of the Buddha, behind a grille, lotus-seated, the room to which the girl took Steiner was almost devoid of furniture. A low table, mats on the floor, flowers in great vases at each corner of the huge picture window with its vista of the night-encumbered mountains to the west. Vague, disturbing perfume—of incense and cooking—filled the air. Steiner waited, expectantly.

'Mr Steiner!' The voice came from somewhere above his head, very close, it seemed, intimate; a little too realistic for a real human voice, and with too much resonance and an excess of sibilance like a hi-fi reproducer with the treble and bass controls turned way up.

'Sit down, Mr Steiner. Your dinner will be served

97

immediately.' The voice was silk-smooth, urbane, precise English with the merest trace of oriental overtone. 'You will forgive me for not joining you?'

Since there was no chair to sit on, Steiner sat down on a mat at the low table. The Chinese girl reappeared with a bowl of pork and *awabi* soup, steaming, fragrant.

Ravenous, Steiner ate his soup.

'To your taste, Mr Steiner?'

'Delicious!' Steiner said, on his best behaviour. 'Really good. Better than anything States-side.'

'That is to be expected! American cooking—even Chinese–American—is indescribable!' The voice shuddered.

Steiner stiffened. He had conditioned reflexes whenever hot dogs were threatened, even by implication.

The voice chuckled. 'I am joking, Mr Steiner. I have enjoyed many excellent meals in America. Forgive, please, the incivility! You must forgive also my not greeting you more personally. It is important you are never able to recognize my face.'

'I understand.'

The girl, kneeling, served the best duck Steiner had ever tasted, the skin crisp, the flesh succulent, the sauce indefinably aromatic and superb.

The bird had been boned and cut into convenient strips. Ignoring the chop-sticks, Steiner used his fingers.

Courteously, the voice remained silent as he ate. The girl brought him hot towels, Japanese-style, and he wiped his hands and face.

'I hope you don't mind my mentioning it,' Steiner said, 'but my wife hasn't eaten anything for around twenty-four hours . . .'

'Don't worry about Mrs Steiner,' the voice said soothingly.

'It's just that she's more than a little touchy. Bracelets she's used to, not handcuffs.'

'I regret they were necessary—for her own protection.'

98

'She's not used to being shot at either. This country's at war—a shooting war—with anyone?'

'Local pinpricks. Guerrilla activity. They seem to know when we are expecting guests—such as yourself—and attempt to take prisoners.'

'They? Who's they?'

'Small bands of mercenaries who work, very unofficially, for the other side. Don't worry, Mr Steiner. We'd never let them take you alive. My men had strict orders to shoot if there was the slightest possibility of capture.'

'They did shoot!'

'Ah, you misunderstood me, Mr Steiner. The orders were, of course, to shoot you.'

Steiner, remembering the hanged men out on the terrace, began to sweat. He dabbed his face with the towel.

The girl glided in with a dish of fruit and scented green tea, then disappeared again, like a green silk shadow. Lit only by candles, the room was filled with shadows.

'Bring your tea over to the screen, Mr Steiner,' the voice said. 'Let us talk seriously.'

Obediently, Steiner rose. Now the daylight had gone, the Buddha was only dimly discernable. Steiner squatted on another mat and waited.

'Good. You are comfortable?'

The voice, instead of coming from the hi-fi system, unreal, impersonal, was now perfectly human and coming from an identified source. The Buddha. The statue had become a man.

A man who said, 'The image I have replaced has for me no particular ideological or religious significance, Mr Steiner. It is simply something that pleases me, aesthetically, and is of the East rather than the West. Nothing more.'

Steiner could not make out the other's features behind the grille. In the increasing darkness of the room, the atmosphere was now enclosed, claustrophobic, heavily charged like that of a confessional.

The image said, 'First, my compliments. The information you have passed to us over the last six months has proved reliable and useful. That from Spain, Belgium, France, Britain, the United States particularly so. The courier system appears to be working satisfactorily. Peking is satisfied.'

Gratified to receive the approbation of the god, Steiner said, 'It's nice to be appreciated.'

'You receive two thousand dollars a month plus expenses,' the god said. 'It is your duty to give satisfaction. Have you any conception what two thousand dollars means in China, not just in a month, or a year, or a life-time?'

'I'm not living in China,' Steiner said. 'I'm a mercenary, working on your side. Strictly for hire.' It was necessary to start the way you meant to go on. No nonsense. This chink playing Buddha didn't scare him.

'You're threatening me? Hinting that you could go over to the other side for more money?' The tone was surprised.

'No. But in the world we're living in that sort of thing isn't exactly unknown.'

'You are a very intelligent and also a very stupid man, Mr Steiner,' the god said, 'which is one of the reasons why I decided to have a look at you myself, instead of relying on the reports of the usual contacts. It is very important—for you—that you impress me favourably.'

'You said you were satisfied with the information you'd been getting.'

'With the information, yes. Your conduct, no. You suffer from unfortunate weaknesses of character, particularly as far as women are concerned.'

'Well, now. . . .' Steiner laughed his man-of-the-world laugh. 'A man can't live by bread alone. Any little adventures I have—very discreet, always with girls who couldn't possibly present a security risk—pick-ups!'

'Those "pick-ups", Mr Steiner, are the most dangerous of all to a man in your position—to whom almost nothing happens by chance.'

The encounter in Corfu! Steiner opened his mouth, said nothing.

'Precisely!' the god said, reading his thoughts. 'You are lucky to be here at all. Lucky to have escaped with just a few scratches on the face, and a severe, but I hope salutary, shock!'

'That girl I picked up in Kerkira! An agent, working for the other side?'

'The girl wasn't working for the other side. She was working for me!'

'For you? But she tried to kill me!'

'Those were her instructions. If she had succeeded and returned here that would have been sufficient proof that you had become a dangerous liability, best disposed of as quickly as possible. As it was, you killed her—which indicates to me that, in spite of being several pounds overweight—you are not as slow, physically and mentally, as may at first seem.'

'You sent that girl just to see what would happen?'

'To test your resourcefulness in an emergency. That was one reason. To prove to you that *all* contacts are potentially dangerous. The second reason was a little more devious.'

'I'm all ears,' said Steiner.

'It would be better if you were all brain,' the god returned.

'The girl, too, was being tested. She was told you were a hostile agent and ordered to kill you, and failed! Being dead, she is now of no importance—except of course to you. Make a nuisance of yourself, Mr Steiner, and you can rest assured that you will be charged with her murder.'

For a long moment neither god nor man spoke. Then Steiner said, 'I need a woman now and then. All right! So I'm a married man. But have you seen Mrs Steiner?'

'I have indeed seen Mrs Steiner,' the god said in a low voice, 'and I sympathize. I realize you are handicapped by Mrs Steiner. I also realize she holds you in perpetual terror, psychological, physical, financial. I know she has more than a hundred thousand dollars in the first National Bank—and another fifty thousand in Switzerland. . . .'

Steiner was about to say something, but the god gestured him into silence. 'You are about to say, "Where would I get one hundred and fifty thousand dollars?" You got them by blackmailing, exacting involuntary contributions from refugees. So be it! Many occupations have their legitimate perquisites—including the occupation of spy. I do not blame you for exacting tribute. But it was a mistake to entrust the funds to your wife.'

Steiner said, 'She thought it would be safer, arouse less suspicion, be more convenient.'

'Certainly, for her. In the event of your death or disappearance. Your wife is a difficult woman. I will do what I can to help you.'

'Help me? About Mrs S.?'

'Let us move on to more important topics,' the god said. 'For example, Otto Hagmann.'

'What about Hagmann? He did his job in London, perfectly. No hitch; a model operation.'

'Except that the surgeon has vanished.'

Steiner was silent for a moment. This was news! He had not been in touch with his office for some days. 'Perhaps he's taking a vacation. He's been under a strain.'

'No one vanishes from my sight, Mr Steiner,' the god said. 'You were taking a vacation in Corfu. Did I lose sight of you, day or night?'

Steiner began to sweat a little.

'Tell me,' the god continued, 'what is your assessment of Hagmann?'

'A cool, reliable killer.'

'Reliable? A moment ago you said he had been under a strain. He has been drinking?'

'Some. Not enough to impair his efficiency.'

'Alcohol invariably impairs efficiency. Including your

own. But at least you have the sense to limit your consumption of bourbon whisky to your hotel room at night—you have been careless with empty bottles. Suppose,' the god continued, 'suppose your protégé has been captured. Would he talk?'

'Isn't there a point where everyone talks, with the right kind of unfriendly persuasion?'

'I'm glad you recognize that. Remember Hagmann is one of the earliest members of your group. He knows a great deal. He could be very dangerous. That is why *you* have to find him.'

'But I'm administrative,' Steiner protested. 'Chief Executive.'

'Executive. Exactly, Mr Steiner. You will find Hagmann, and execute him.'

'Me?'

'Personally. In Corfu you showed the necessary talent.'

'But Hagmann is one of our best men. He's resourceful, shows initiative. It's possible he's pursuing some useful investigation of his own right now.'

'The subject is closed,' the god said. 'Hagmann has become unreliable. He will therefore be eliminated. A salutary lesson for every member of the Organization to ponder. Including yourself, Mr Steiner. We will now turn to the next topic. The scheduled assassination of the American military person. Please give me your report on arrangements so far made. . . .'

It was two hours before Steiner got back to his own room. Most of the time had been devoted to a discussion of practical details, but he had also to suffer an ideological lecture. China was now the sole reliable representative of world Communism. In large parts of Asia success in the struggle was already within sight. There were stirrings in South America. In Africa the day would surely come when the black masses turned decisively to Peking for help. But the greatest triumph of all would be in Europe—a triumph for which it was the splendid duty of their particular organization to pave the way. . . .

Steiner had also been allowed a glimpse of himself, in perhaps ten years time: commissar, leader of men, one before whom those who were left of the old régimes—politicians, bureaucrats, prelates, generals, captains of commerce and industry—would tremble. . . . A reward for his faithful services to the cause.

The prospect was, of course, pleasing, but at the moment the thought of three fingers of bourbon even more so, sipped slowly after a shower, followed by . . .

Steiner let his eye wander over the boyishly slim figure of the Chinese girl who had, evidently, been assigned to look after him. A cute little thing, smelling vaguely of sandalwood. She had a way of looking at him from beneath lashes that promised a lot of fun.

The girl led him back the way he had come, up a staircase, along a white-painted unfurnished corridor—featureless except for half a dozen closed and presumably locked doors. Steiner wondered if there were any other 'guests'. There was no sign of them. The girl unlocked the door to his room and stood aside, head lowered.

'Effie!' he called.

The bedroom was empty, the bathroom, too. Also, the place was tidy. Whenever his wife occupied a room for more than a few minutes there was inevitably a litter of clothes on every chair, toilet articles spread over every available square inch, drip-dries dripping away in the bathroom.

Now, the place was as impersonal and tidy as an hotel room after the chambermaids had cleared up after the departed guests.

Then the explanation suddenly occurred to him.

'Hey!' he said, grinning, to the Chinese girl, 'you brought me to the wrong room.'

The girl smiled back. 'No, no. Light room!' she lisped. 'You see.'

She opened the built-in cupboard. His light-weights were neatly arranged on hangers, shirts, socks and underwear in the drawers provided.

Steiner spun round, puzzled. 'Mrs Steiner!' he said. 'What happened to her? All her things?'

The girl shook her head, charmingly anxious, but unable to help.

'Not understand,' she said. 'So sorry.'

'My wife! Where is she? She's been put in another room?'

The girl went on smiling, shaking her head.

Steiner started again, slowly, as if to a child. 'The lady who arrived with me . . . *La signora* . . . *die dame* . . . *ma femme*. . . .' He was struggling to remember the word for wife in Greek when the phone beside the bed rang.

Steiner grabbed the instrument. He recognized the voice. Naturally. He had been listening to it for more than three hours.

'Mr Steiner,' the god said, 'don't be concerned about your wife.'

'I'm not exactly concerned. Just puzzled. From where I'm standing it looks like instant divorce.'

'Are you complaining, Mr Steiner, with what you see from where you're standing?'

The god had a smile in his voice. Steiner involuntarily looked around the room. What he saw from where he was standing was the girl, and she had already unzipped her dress. She held the garment against her, lightly, demurely, with both hands. A tiny movement of the fingers and it would drop to her feet.

Steiner lost his voice.

'Her name is Mia Hahn, which means Precious Emerald. This girl, I assure you, has no knife or any other deadly weapon concealed about her person. This will be made plain to you in the clearest possible way.'

105

Exactly on cue, the delicate fingers of the girl fluttered. She stepped out of the dress and turned slowly, demurely, like an exquisite doll, for his inspection.

'You are satisfied, Mr Steiner?'

Steiner found his voice. 'Perfectly.'

'Good. Do not waste precious moments by questioning the girl about your wife, about this place, about me. She will talk to you about nothing except love.'

A click and the line went dead.

'Mia Hahn,' he said.

The girl bowed prettily.

'Precious Emerald! Well, that's quite a name!'

Steiner moved towards her, unconsciously licking his somewhat fleshy lips.

Chapter Twelve

Stimulated by his interesting labours of the night and with a high opinion of at least one aspect of Chinese culture, the following evening found Steiner back in Frankfurt.

The journey out of Albania had been considerably less adventurous than the one in. Helicopter, without Mrs S., of course, to Tirana; then a noisy ride in an ancient piston-engined bomber with no hostess, no lavatory, no proper seats, no heating and a Bulgarian crew to Sofia, where he caught a K.L.M. Boeing 707 homeward bound from the Far East. Excellent lunch, attentive service.

Steiner arrived at his office in Frankfurt just off the Habsburger Allee soothed, confident and cosseted, like any other executive back at base after a satisfactory pow-wow at head office.

Fräulein Reiss, his personal private secretary, rose politely to greet him as he entered the outer office.

'You had a pleasant vacation, Mr Steiner?' She spoke American with only the faintest trace of German accent. She had worked three years for PX in Heidelberg, after careful screening for possible Nazi activities during the war, and then after further careful screening had been seconded to the C.I.A.

Steiner knowing she was an agent set to watch over him, felt flattered and relieved. As long as she was his secretary, turning in her painstaking reports on his various contacts and business activities, all was well. He did his best to keep her interested, but unsuspicious. When he went out for lunch he would leave drawers that should have been locked, open; let remarks slip that might mean something, take her into his confidence about matters that could have been safely screamed from the housetops.

Fräulein Reiss was, naturally, extremely interested in his innumerable international contacts. So interested that he felt certain the day wasn't far off when he would be approached with a view to acting for C.I.A. himself! An amusing, but dangerous, idea. The Chinese would definitely not understand the delicacy of his position.

'Mrs Steiner's feeling rested?' Fräulein Reiss put on an ecstatic expression. 'Oh, to be in the south at this time of the year!'

'Mrs Steiner is enjoying it so much, she's staying on a little longer.' A vacation from your wife, that's what the god had said—not a permanent separation. Steiner was grateful.

'Wonderful!' Fräulein Reiss fluttered her eyelashes and heaved her ample bosom, one of her most irritating mannerisms. His senses still tuned to the charms of Precious Emerald, Steiner turned away with distaste, sat at his desk and leafed through the pile of more urgent correspondence placed before him.

For several minutes he dealt with unimportant matters. Then, when the word 'London' was mentioned, he said, as if the thought had only that moment occurred to him, 'Ah, yes, London! If Herr Hagmann is in the office you might ask him to come and see me.'

'But the telegram, Herr Steiner! The telegram!'

It was among the documents she had placed before him, only a few of which he had bothered to read. He now did so.

108

It had been sent from London three days previously, was addressed to him personally.

REGRET INFORM YOU OTTO HAGMANN SUFFERED HEART ATTACK.
PLEASE CONTACT MEDICAL REGISTRAR ST MICHAEL'S HOSPITAL LONDON.

Steiner said nothing for a moment, which Fräulein Reiss attributed, quite naturally, to shock, even grief. Actually, he was thinking. About Hagmann's medical record. Hagmann drank, he smoked, he ate. Too much of all three. Twenty-thirty pounds overweight maybe. But he was also a man who kept in shape. He took exercise (boxing and wrestling), he was quick on his feet, his reactions split-second fast. A heart attack?

Steiner weighed the possibility, the genuineness of the telegram. Also he was concerned about the possible far-too-revealing utterances of a sick man. The recent case of Briantanu and his impending nervous breakdown in the States came vividly to mind.

Being human, he was also concerned about himself. Hell, anyone could have a coronary. But he was also relieved. If Hagmann died of natural causes, he wouldn't have to kill him.

'Poor guy!' he permitted himself to say, at last. 'Hagmann! Well, well!' Then, more briskly, since after all, as far as Fräulein Reiss was concerned, Hagmann was merely an employee of the Organization. 'You contacted this hospital?'

'The moment we received the telegram, Herr Direktor! And again this morning. Not half an hour before you arrived.'

'Well?'

'They said a relative should go over there as quickly as possible.'

'Hagmann doesn't have any relatives?'

109

'There are none listed on our records, Herr Direktor.'

Steiner stared at the ceiling, then took an immaculate handkerchief from his pocket and dabbed his eyes. 'It's a shock, Fräulein Reiss! Herr Hagmann is a most valued member of our Organization. What else did the hospital say?' It was an emotional moment.

'He's on the danger list. They would say nothing definite, of course, but when it's the heart . . . anything . . .'

Fräulein Reiss permitted herself a great sob, this time the kind she usually reserved for a climax in Wagner.

Of one thing Steiner was convinced. It was absolutely necessary to see Hagmann himself.

'Fräulein Reiss,' he said, 'please get me a seat on the first available plane for London.'

Less than four hours later, Steiner was staring at the face of Hagmann. Eyes closed, utterly inscrutable, a private face, beyond all intrusion. A dead face, in the hospital mortuary.

In a neighbouring room, via a hidden microphone, Sarratt and Anna listened.

'When did he die?'

'Two hours ago. Quite suddenly. He seemed better. And then. . . . A second attack in such cases . . .'

In fact, Hagmann had been in a refrigerator for over a week.

'I understand.'

The mortuary attendant's manner was perfect. Why not? He knew nothing. The Medical Superintendent, however, was a little nervous. To assert that a man with two bullets in him had died of a heart attack. . . . If the directive had not come from the highest possible source, he would have refused to be a party to—well, whatever it was.

'There will be an inquest?'

The Medical Superintendent shook his head. 'As the patient was admitted to hospital more than twenty-four hours before death, that will not be necessary . . .' He dabbed his forehead. 'The cause of death is not in doubt.'

Steiner was aware of the official's nervousness, and puzzled. Why should he be nervous? An occurrence of this kind must, after all, be mere routine.

'He collapsed at his hotel?'

'In the street.' The M.S. referred to his records (or rather, to his directive). 'We were able to trace his business address by finding a return air ticket on him. His passport, of course, was in his pocket. The authorities collected his luggage from the airline's terminal.'

Luggage! For a moment, Steiner was seriously worried. Suppose the gun—the weapon that had murdered H'an Yang—was among Hagmann's things!

'I can have possession of his effects?'

'I see no objection.'

Steiner felt reassured. No police, no awkward questions, no departure from what, he imagined, was normal routine.

'You wish the body to be returned to Germany?' The M.S. was saying diffidently, though this was in fact a crucial question. Once the body was exported, the true cause of death would certainly emerge. However, he was merely obeying instructions.

Instructions from Sarratt, who was playing a hunch. Surely Steiner would want official form-filling, inquiries, formalities of every kind to be as brief as possible!

The hunch was right. Steiner said, 'There's no objection to burial in this country?'

'Cremation, if you wish.'

So be it! The less of Hagmann that remained, Steiner figured, the better. A handful of dust. Fine! Scatter it to the four winds!

The formalities were quickly arranged. An undertaker, a date, even an announcement in *The Times* . . . 'no flowers . . .'

The Times announcement was a good idea. It would reassure the god in his Albanian heaven, convince him

Steiner's mission had been accomplished. If the god thought that he, Steiner, was able to contrive a death by natural causes, so much the better.

Two gods instead of one! Steiner had no doubt copies of *The Times* reached Albania by the usual route.

While waiting for the funeral, Steiner checked in at a quiet hotel in a backwater just behind Piccadilly. Green Park seemed especially green; it was pleasant to stroll in St James's, take mid-morning coffee at Fortnum's, watch the women, anticipate lunch at Bentley's.

A visit to London had been 'on' anyway. Naturally Steiner was interested in *émigré* artists.

He was received with especial cordiality, even deference, at the Gallery Maribor, run by a couple named Gora who had come to Britain from Yugoslavia during the Second World War. Gora, an unsuccessful artist, had been about to leave the art world altogether and open a bistro when Steiner appeared on the scene and announced that the Organization was prepared to finance Gora to open an art gallery to specialize in the work of refugee painters.

So Gora caught the upswing of the post-war art boom. He had an instinctive flair for the kind of pictures that would sell, even if he couldn't paint them himself. Within a year, he had moved to an expensive flat in Park Lane whose walls were graced by the best of his stock of paintings, and gave lavish parties to industrialists, politicians and the diplomatic set that became famous.

At these parties were also carefully selected members of Gora's stable of artists, all hungry, all of whose politics were elastic. The kind of men who would get themselves invited to the right houses, the right receptions. Gora soon became one of the most effective spy-masters in London—with tentacles that reached all over the Western world.

His artists travelled. They collected information which, via Gora, found its way to Steiner.

Mrs Gora, now expensively dressed in a model day-dress

from Harrods, served Steiner coffee in the office. He noticed her hand shook. Her nervous system had never fully recovered from the strain of those early years.

'You've been ill again?'

'No, no. It's nothing.'

Her husband carefully fitted a Turkish cigarette into a fine amber holder. 'A little insomnia. The old trouble. You know how it is.'

'Which doctor?'

'Doctor?'

'She takes pills, doesn't she? Something for the insomnia? Something to calm her down?'

'Naturally.'

'So?'

'I get the pills for her. Personally. Don't worry.' Gora lit his cigarette with an 18-carat gold lighter, and inhaled deeply. With affluence he had put on weight, become smug, self-confident. Now the risks of the game seemed to worry him not at all. Perhaps, Steiner reflected, he was a little too nonchalant.

'*I* don't worry,' Steiner said. '*You* should!'

In a desperate attempt at conversation, Mrs Gora burst out, 'How is Mrs Steiner? Isn't she with you on this trip?'

'Mrs Steiner hasn't been feeling too well, either,' he said casually. 'We all have these little health problems.'

Mrs Gora went into the gallery to talk to a client.

When they were alone, Gora said, 'She isn't always like this. She doesn't really *know* anything . . . hasn't for years. She just helps in the business, and I mean the business. That's all.'

Steiner smiled affably, nodding his head, waiting for the other to finish. Then he stopped nodding, stopped smiling, and said, 'She knows you.'

'You're saying I can't control my own wife?' Gora was a big man in the Organization. He didn't like being talked to this way, not even by Steiner.

113

'That remains to be seen,' Steiner was smiling again. 'Nervous breakdowns mean psychiatrists, sodium pentothal, hypnosis. Those are risks we don't take. Do something.'

Gora chewed his lower lip, made no comment.

'Now,' Steiner said. 'About Hagmann.'

'Well, he came to see me. Naturally.'

'And you talked about what?'

'*Business*, business. Pictures. Artists. Diplomatic chit-chat.'

'Such as?'

'A certain American major passing through London on his way to a semi-political appointment in Ankara is a homosexual. A certain Rumanian diplomat based here becomes dangerously—but usefully—indiscreet when drunk—which is almost every evening. He fears he is about to be recalled. The situation has possibilities.' Gora lit another cigarette. 'I'll give you the details.'

'Later. How did Hagmann act?'

'Like his usual self. Possibly not so relaxed.'

That was understandable, with the killing of H'an Yang on his mind. But Gora knew nothing of Hagmann's most important assignment in London. No executive knew more than was good for him about the activities of the Organization as a whole. Even today, fifteen years on the pay-roll, Gora was not certain the Chinese were his real masters.

'He looked ill?'

'Like a man about to have a heart attack? No, he didn't. But what does that mean. I played golf with a man last year, a client, a man in the War Office. Very useful. The fifth hole—all of four hundred and fifty yards. He drove off, a beauty, right down the middle of the fairway, and the ball landed within three iron range of the green. A birdie for sure. Except he was dead. Before the ball even landed.' Gora tapped his own chest. 'Who's to know? That man had passed an insurance doctor the week before!'

Steiner winced, involuntarily. Sometimes he worried

about his own health. One day perhaps it would all end—doped to stupefaction, in a hospital bed—or just out—puff! Like a snuffed candle.

'Of course he was drinking,' Gora said. 'But you know Hagmann—after a whole bottle, solo, he never looked drunk.'

'So nothing about him struck you as strange, peculiar? He did nothing, nothing at all, that seemed odd, unexplained?'

Gora shook his head. 'I only saw him twice. The second time he seemed especially interested in the newspapers. But that was the day the Chinese was assassinated, so. . . .'

Gora broke off. Of course! Between the murder and Hagmann, there must be a connexion. Why hadn't the idea occurred to him before? But it would be idiotic to let Steiner know what he suspected. A sentence of death. His face was mask-like.

'But of course nobody talked of anything else. As I was saying, he just sat in that chair, reading the *Evening Standard*—filled with the story of the assassination, the demonstrators at the cemetery. In that very chair. . . . It might have been that lunch edition.'

Steiner's eye fell on a copy of the *Standard*. The lead story was cricket. But prominent, just below the fold, was a headline that riveted his attention.

BODY UNDER BED. SURPRISE FOR BRITISH HONEYMOON COUPLE ON HOLIDAY ISLE.

He picked up the paper.
The dateline was Corfu.
'*On this sun-drenched holiday isle of Corfu, Mr and Mrs Rankin, married only forty-eight hours, checked into a waterfront hotel. They were given Room Number 17. After she had unpacked her trousseau, Mrs Alice Rankin tried to push her suitcase under the bed. . . .*'

Gora was saying, 'Surely you don't suspect what the British call "foul play".'

115

'What?' Steiner's eyes remained fixed on the news story. 'I mean if the hospital authorities say he died of heart failure . . .'

' . . . *The identity of the dead woman remains a mystery. . . . Was this a sex killing? The local police are uncommunicative. If this is merely a sordid waterfront crime, why the official silence? Why have police officers from Athens moved in? Meanwhile, Mr and Mrs Rankin, shaken, but not unduly depressed by the experience, continue their honeymoon—at another hotel. . . .*'

Steiner put the newspaper aside. Clearly, the god was allowing just as much 'evidence' to reach the Greek police as suited his purpose. One step out of line and he was a candidate for a cell in an Athens jail. Unless, of course, they had capital punishment in Greece.

He took a handkerchief and dabbed his forehead. 'Heart failure. . . . Anyone . . .'

'Exactly!' Gora said. 'Nothing to worry about. Now let me tell you about the American major heading for Ankara. . . .'

Anna had been issued with the standard one thousand dollars' worth of mixed West European currencies. Her clothes were impersonal, the labels New York. Macy's. Saks. The usual places, for anyone, everyone. The outfits were cute, anyway, and she enjoyed wearing them. A slick chick! Now it was a question of timing.

She had taken coffee at Fortnum's, allowing him to catch only the merest glimpse of her hidden behind the Paris edition of the *Herald-Tribune*. He had obviously something on his mind. He wasn't interested. Good. A woman to be vaguely recognized should emerge not from the precise, but the misty past.

She did not stay at the same hotel. Too obvious! Nor did she follow his every movement—the visit to the tailor just off Savile Row, for instance, whose head cutter, as it happened, had been interesting M.I.6 for some little time. It

116

was possible Steiner was merely a customer, anyway—the firm had a large international clientele.

The three days before Hagmann's funeral he occupied with blameless, even laudable activities. As principal executive of the Organization he attended a concert given by a Polish cellist, was guest of honour at a dinner party, his host being the secretary of a well-known literary club.

The cremation took place at Golders Green, a brief non-denominational service attended by Steiner and half a dozen of Hagmann's business and Organization contacts—giving Steiner moral support. 'Valued colleague,' he was heard to say. 'Almost irreplaceable.' The slight catch in his voice was good theatre.

So it was that the mortal remains of Otto Hagmann, spy and murderer, were reduced to dust, like those of any honest man.

Anna waited at her hotel. Since leaving the studio, she had not returned to her flat. Anna Zordan had, for this assignment at least, ceased to exist. Her last act in the Zordan skin had been to phone her agent, Bill Kraster.

Target Films, she said, with appropriate excitement, liked her, had offered her a part in a movie to be shot on various Continental locations. The money was good. And Bill, of course, was also happy. He would draw his ten per cent.

Anna put down the receiver and contemplated the new girl in the hotel mirror. The Christian name was still Anna. But her new U.S. passport said her surname was O'Connor.

In the mirror, what did she see? A stranger? Not exactly. Perhaps a cousin. Hair a shade lighter, restyled to sweep back over the head, caught at the nape in a ribbon. Lips painted on less full lines, but more make-up than before, especially on the cheek-bones. Her face seemed thinner. Now she wore glasses, which gave her an intent, serious, post-graduate look.

A good job, in double quick time, had been done by the studio's dramatic coach, a small, bird-like woman who had

117

once taught at a well-known stage school in New York. A personality transference. Now Anna was able to identify herself almost completely with a certain real girl about whom, it was hoped, all relevant facts were known—twenty-four-year old, recently resident in Washington, D.C., niece of a well-known Senator, just embarking on a six-months grand tour of Europe, partly to help her get over an unhappy love affair, partly because she hoped to take up journalism as a career. A girl Steiner had once met.

This new Anna was more inhibited than the old one, more vulnerable, sensitive. Useful qualities that would help to mask the strangeness, to disarm suspicion. The new Anna was also provocative. Without the provocation, Sarratt had decided, Steiner just wouldn't be interested. The provocation got past the glasses very successfully.

To get in the right frame of mind, for the last three days she had been catching up on the exhibitions at the various London galleries, the Summer Exhibition at the Royal Academy, the Tate. She had been to the National Theatre and the Mermaid, eaten at several of the best West End restaurants to get the feel of her Diner's Club Credit Card. Most of the time she had gone around with a girl from San Francisco named Honey chummed up with during an American Express coach trip to Windsor. It helped her try out her role and perfect it, also provided some solace against loneliness.

In the Mirabelle, just as she and Honey were moving from the bar to their table, they ran straight into a young man she had seen a good deal of once—before the last trip to Vienna and the world fell in.

Their eyes met. He was going to speak, then thought better of it when he saw the total unrecognition on Anna's face. He moved on and she heard the redhead he was with say 'All right, darling, she *was* pretty, in a sort of bluestocking way. But you are a bit of a swine to give her such a going over—I mean after last night. . . .'

It was a good test. She had been friendly with Johnnie almost, but not quite to the point of sleeping with him.

This incident was before the funeral. The following day, an hour after Hagmann had been reduced to dust by the quick, hygienic, modern method, she was in her hotel room, as arranged, at noon.

The phone rang. A man's voice said, 'Miss O'Connor?'

'Yeah. Sure.'

'Oh, this is the travel agency,' the voice said, 'just to confirm you're booked on Lufthansa Flight 245 to Frankfurt this evening at five o'clock from London Airport. A messenger will deliver your ticket to your hotel.'

So this was it. During the last war, outgoing spies and agents from England usually landed on Continental Europe by parachute. Now, apparently, you travelled like any tourist. She had wondered, briefly, about how her transfer to the unknown would be managed—with a morbid curiosity like a condemned prisoner concerned about the mechanism of the drop, the precise mechanics of execution. This was too easy, too comfortable, cocooned, cosseted, encapsulated.

Chapter Thirteen

Anna and Steiner travelled by the same plane. This was, of course, intentional. If, subsequently, he did begin to think he had seen her before—well, he had! A little necessary conditioning.

In the aircraft, he sat a little in front of her, across the gangway, drank coffee, glanced at *Encounter*, *The Economist* and *Paris Match*, dozed, repelled his neighbour's efforts at conversation.

At the Frankfurt terminal, he collected his baggage, hailed a taxi and was gone. Anna also took a taxi, checked into the Intercontinental on the Bürgerstrasse (it was nice that basic expenses were fifty dollars a day). She opened the bottle of Scotch she had prudently bought duty free on the plane, sent for a bucket of ice, peeled off her clothes and stepped under the shower, starting warm, then turned to cold.

She took her time, guessing Steiner would be similarly occupied. Then she carefully checked the number of his private apartment she had been given with the directory, and gave it to the operator.

He answered almost at once. '*Ja?*'

'Herr Steiner . . . oh, *Mr* Steiner . . .' She gave a little deprecating giggle. 'Do you mind if we talk English . . . I

mean, fellow-Americans. . . . And *Wiener Schnitzel* is just
about the only thing I can say in German, anyway!' She
hoped her voice sounded sufficiently naïve, girlish and sexy
not to make him hang up.

'Okay,' he said, 'let's talk English. Who is this?'

'Well, you won't remember me, Mr Steiner. But perhaps
my name's familiar to you. It's O'Connor. Anna O'Connor.'

'No, I don't know anyone of that name. What can I do
for you, anyway?'

'Well, it's like this, Mr Steiner. I'm a sort of journalist,
and I'd be very grateful if you'd give me an interview.'

'No, that's something I don't do, Miss O'Connor. You *did*
say Miss?'

'I didn't, but I'm a Miss, anyway, because I'm concen-
trating on my career—and your saying "no" like that isn't
helping my career one tiny bit, Mr Steiner.' She put a
plaintive note into her voice. 'You won't change your
mind?'

'No. I'm sorry.'

'If not for my sake, then for uncle's?'

'Uncle? Who's uncle?'

'The Senator. Edmund Jefferson O'Connor.'

Brief pause. 'The Senator's your uncle?'

'Why, certainly! That's why I said my name might be
familiar. Uncle said, "When you go to Europe, be sure to
look up my friend Ed Steiner. If anyone can give you
the right kind of help, contacts and show you around,
it's Ed!"'

Into another fifteen seconds of silence Steiner put a great
deal of concentrated thought. The Senator was prominent
on the Foreign Relations Committee. The Senator had
personally convinced many citizens and business firms that
the causes of patriotism, tax-avoidance and business self-
interest (by protecting the American way of life against the
Reds) could be simply and neatly served by a cheque made
out to the Organization. It was, indirectly, thanks to the

121

Senator that Mrs Steiner possessed a balance of something like half a million Swiss francs in Zürich.

To rebuff the niece of such a sponsor would be plain lunacy.

'Are you there, Mr Steiner?'

'Still with you, Miss O'Connor.' He put a smile and becoming modesty into his voice. 'It's my policy never to attract personal publicity.'

'But without dedicated men like you . . .'

'Just a humble servant, Miss O'Connor. But why not come and see me? I'd be very happy to see and talk to the niece of the man who's done so much more for the movement than I. At my apartment? Tomorrow at eleven o'clock?'

Anna hung up, excited, gratified. So far so good. He had found time for her, and, if Sarratt's suspicions were correct, Steiner must have a lot on his mind.

Because in exactly five days' time, the second victim, key politician in SEATO—General Aloysius Wilberforce Duncan Grant—was due to die.

General Aloysius Wilberforce Grant, aged sixty, U.S. Army retired, a dollar-a-year trouble-shooter and personal representative of the President of the United States, had been shot at many times in his life. But he didn't seem unduly concerned that he might be shot at again.

'Though of course,' as Sarratt told him, 'we have no means of knowing the assassin will use a gun.'

The General, Sarratt and a C.I.A. man named Garris were seated on the patio of the rather splendid villa that had been rented for the General on the outskirts of Rangoon. The villa had been taken because the General's mission had turned out to be far more protracted than had at first been surmised. Grant didn't mind this. He found the country fascinating, the people charming, and had even taken to wearing the *gaungbaung*, a kind of light turban, to show that he was a man whose heart, at least, was in the right place.

'Assassinated!' he said again. 'But I'm one of the most popular men in the country. The government like me, even the opposition. Even the British.' He poured out another round of gin and tonic, genuinely puzzled. The General had reduced popularity to a science. Knowingly, he had never given personal offence to anyone. And not just because he used the right deodorant. In Bonn, Paris, London, Ankara, Madrid, Bombay, Teheran and a dozen other cities in the last year or so, he had demonstrated, like a one-man commercial, that personal affability worked, it sold the U.S.A.

His methods even worked in the United States itself. Even in Texas. Especially in Texas, since the General was a Texan himself. Now he was a little irked because Sarratt, a Limey for Chrissake, seemed impervious to the famous charm.

Sarratt said patiently, 'It's nothing personal, General. These people simply have to prove to their own Party, to their followers all over the world, and of course to themselves, that their methods, their organization work. Otherwise, they're out of business.'

'They probably took your name out of a hat, sir,' Garris said. 'Anyway, our information is that these murders are scheduled to take place at precise intervals. They'll do everything possible to kill you on schedule. To prove they're infallible.'

'And you're here to protect me?'

'Well, yes and no, sir,' Garris said. 'Unless we flew you back States-side in an army bomber and locked you up in San Quentin in a maximum security cell, we couldn't guarantee to protect you. If a public man goes on appearing in public, well, we and the T-men can do *something* to protect him, but in the face of a determined, unknown killer, often it's not enough. John Kennedy, Dallas, 1963.'

Garris got up and looked out over the garden where a

native was watering the brilliantly flowering shrubs. A pea-
cock uttered a shrill cry. There must have been twenty of
them in the garden. Now it was approaching roosting-
time. One after another, in some secret order of priority,
ungainly and a little absurd, they fluttered from the ground
first to a low wall, then on to a rain-tree, where each bird
took up its accustomed perch. The tree was heavy with
them. In the fading light they looked menacing, Garris
thought, like vultures.

'The gardener had his tongue cut out by the Japanese
in 1944,' the General broke the silence. 'I hardly think he's
your man.'

'Yes, we know that,' the C.I.A. man said. 'All the members of your staff here, inside and out, seem perfectly reliable.' He hesitated, a little uncomfortably. 'The thing is,
sir, our instructions are *not* to protect you. The idea is the
attempt on your life must take place.'

The General thought for a moment, carefully examining
the end of his cheroot. 'That can only mean one thing. You
don't know who you are up against, what organization.'

'Exactly,' Sarratt said. 'We have certain suspicions, not a
shred of proof. We've got to have the assassin alive.'

'The would-be assassin!' the General corrected.

'Of course we do hope to catch him in time, sir. But until
he shows himself . . .' Garris coughed and made a vague
gesture.

'What it boils down to is simply this: I'm a live target.
Expendable.'

'You would have protection. As much as possible without
arousing suspicion.'

There was a longish silence. Then Garris said, 'I have the
President's authority, sir, to tell you that an army plane is at
your immediate disposal. We arrived here in a car, built
like a tank, made of bullet-proof glass and heavy-guage
steel. You could be on your way to the airport and then to
the States in a matter of minutes, where you would be given

124

maximum security treatment for as long as you wish. If necessary, for life. Also, the President ordered me to tell you that if you decide to accept this offer, your decision will never be divulged to anyone.'

The General laughed. 'Meaning no one except you two and the President of the United States would know I'm chicken! Well, gentlemen, it's an intriguing proposition. Frankly, on this assignment I've been bored. Too much smooth talk, too many diplomatic smiles. I was happier in North Africa, Italy, Normandy, Korea, Vietnam.'

'Then you should be happy again now, General,' Sarratt said. 'We think the real enemy this time are Chinese, too.'

'You're a Limey, aren't you? I thought the British were friends of China. Like with Cuba.'

'Speaking for myself, sir,' Sarratt said carefully, 'I deal in the hard facts of a war that is never declared, doesn't officially exist and goes on for ever. The war of spies. I don't have any friends. Friends can be dangerous.'

'Colleagues?' The General glanced from Sarratt to Garris. 'Allies?'

'There are arrangements,' Garris said.

'For mutual convenience,' Sarratt added.

The General grimaced. 'It's not my kind of war, gentlemen. Too devious. I was at West Point, and in my day there the general notion was that war and soldiering could be properly undertaken by a man of honour.' He glanced quickly at them. 'No offence.'

'None taken, sir,' Garris said.

'Perhaps the kind of things you're mixed up in are necessary. I wouldn't know. But personally I prefer things more clear-cut. Strictly off the record, I'd have blasted China to hell years ago. I'm one of *that* particular clique in the Pentagon.'

'Well, it's arguable, sir, that our kind of activities may help to prevent war,' Sarratt said mildly. 'If the intelligence forces of the world reach a kind of stalemate, perhaps some politicians will get the message it just isn't worth while. Generals, too. No offence?'

'None taken,' the General said. 'But war's my profession, not a dirty word.'

Garris glanced uncomfortably at Sarratt and got up. 'Well, sir, thank you for sparing us so much of your time. As I said, the car's at your disposal.'

Sarratt also stood up.

The General made no move, except to ring a small silver bell.

A native servant entered almost at once, carrying an odd-looking fruit on a handsome silver plate. The fruit was round, about the size of a large coconut except that, instead of being smooth the husk was covered with tubercles, each ending in a formidable point.

'You have taken no refreshment, gentlemen,' the General said. 'I really must insist.'

'That's very civil of you, sir,' Sarratt said. He and Garris sat down again.

At a sign from the General, the servant took a large knife and started to open the fruit.

'You're familiar with the famous durian?' the General said to Sarratt. 'It's cultivated in this country. A great favourite of mine. A great delicacy.'

'No. This is my first visit here.'

The General nodded affably. 'There's some wonderful fruit here. Red bananas, papayas, ramosteens, pomeloes. But this one beats the lot.'

Sarratt and Garris watched curiously as the servant deftly opened the fruit.

Immediately the two halves were exposed a nauseating smell filled the room. The General gestured the servant away.

'Now, gentlemen!'

Sarratt felt sick. The smell reminded him of rotten onions,

or worse—even decayed animal matter. He glanced at Garris's face. The C.I.A. man had turned green.

The General seemed unaware that anything was amiss. His expression remained that of a solicitous host. He handed a half to each of his guests. Holding his breath Sarratt saw that the fruit consisted of oval compartments, each filled with a milky-coloured glutinous pulp.

'The pulp's the edible part,' the General said. 'You'll also find seeds, but they're rather hard and are usually roasted. That's another treat in store.'

'I'm sorry, sir. . . .' Garris began.

'Ah, the odour! You find it a little difficult to take?'

'Frankly, yes, I do, General,' Sarratt said.

'You put me in mind of the time when I was being entertained by an Arab sheik—guest of honour, and all that. I was offered the sheep's eye.'

'You ate it?'

'One doesn't insult a man in his own house—or tent, as it happened to be in that case. You eat his food—and it's very bad form, Limey, even to hint that he may be yellow. Especially when he wears with pride several of his own country's decorations, not to mention . . .'

'The Croix de Guerre and the Military Cross.' Sarratt put in. 'I did bone up on your career before we flew out here. It's simply that we had to warn you that you stand about a ninety per cent chance of not coming out of this alive.'

'I'm beginning to feel old,' the General said. 'A twinge here and there. Mostly psychosomatic, I expect. Too much soft living.'

Suddenly, the General grinned. 'Anyway, when the President calls for a volunteer, that's an order.'

Holding his breath, Sarratt plunged his spoon into the soft pulp of the durian. It was unbelievably delicious.

Steiner's apartment was in a newish block at the Deutsch-Herrn Ufer with a splendid view of the River Main.

Functional, no nonsense furniture. No obvious affluence. The plain, pictureless, white-painted walls hinted at monastic austerity appropriate to the surroundings of one devoted to higher things and good works.

The big desk—chair back to the window with its distracting view—had its in and out tray, tape recorder and phone. Steiner had obviously been recording some directive as the the German housekeeper showed Anna in.

He gave her a wide executive smile, a firm handshake. In the opaque grey eyes she sensed suspicion, perhaps recognition.

'Washington?' he said, probing, 'one of your uncle's parties? The best in the Western Hemisphere.'

Anna laughed. 'Maybe. But more likely the plane—yesterday.'

'Plane?'

'From London. I recognized you. But it wouldn't have been fair to take advantage, would it? I mean, to get away from me you'd have to have jumped.'

Keeping the welcome-to-the-Senator's-niece smile clamped firmly on his face, Steiner took in every detail of her appearance. Every detail checked with the description of the girl he had received from the Senator's own lips the previous evening over the transatlantic telephone.

Of course he had taken the obvious precaution of calling the Senator, just to say how delighted he was to have an opportunity of meeting his niece, but would he be good enough to give him a few facts about the girl. . . . After all, anyone could *say* she was Anna O'Connor. . . . The Senator, who had been approached by the C.I.A, warned to expect just such a call, knew exactly what to say and said it, being a politician, with conviction. He proudly acknowledged Anna as his niece, profusely thanked Steiner in advance for any little thing he could do for her, and hinted that a handsome contribution to the splendid work of the Organization could be expected any day now from a large pharmaceutical firm.

In spite of all this, why was he still suspicious?

Steiner gestured her to a chair and came out from behind his desk.

'So you're a free-lance?'

Anna nodded. 'It's fun choosing your own assignments. But tough. What I need is a really worth-while story. Say, about you.'

'Not about me,' he said modestly. 'I'm unimportant.'

'I mean about the Organization. The people the movement tries to help.'

'You know Europe, Miss O'Connor?'

'Well, I majored in European history. But this is my first trip over.'

'Languages?'

'Just a little French.' She searched his face. 'Not much in the way of qualifications. That's what you're thinking, isn't it? But sometimes ignorance can be a virtue in a reporter.'

'I don't follow.' She had very nice legs, a good figure and a provocative mouth, Steiner thought. It was a pity she was the Senator's niece. Or was it? She could so easily have been yet another emissary sent from Albania. He shivered involuntarily, said with feeling, 'Ignorance can be dangerous.'

'The ignorance of the great American public!' In her eagerness, Anna O'Connor sat forward, breathless in her excitement. 'I'm typical of that public, Mr Steiner. Let me enlighten them. It seems to me as good a time as any to start enlightening people is *now*! Especially now.'

'Why?'

'Isn't there an important executive committee meeting about due?'

Steiner's eyes narrowed, but he kept the smile on his lips. He said pleasantly, 'I don't think you are quite as "ignorant" as you'd have me suppose.'

'Only a little briefing from uncle.' The answering smile was ingenuous, open, trusting, as innocent and transparent as a child's asking for candy.

129

Steiner felt more suspicious than ever. Was it conceivably possible, this girl, like the Italian, had also been sent to test him? By the Senator? But that would make the Senator an ally of the Chinese. An impossible, even ridiculous, notion! One thing was certain : he could refuse the Senator nothing.

He said, 'You must understand, Miss O'Connor, that some of the men and women who will attend the executive committee meeting live dangerous lives. When they chose freedom by escaping to the West, they didn't also choose safety.'

'You mean they could be abducted, even killed, by Communist agents?' Anna looked appropriately horrified.

Steiner nodded. 'That's why we don't exactly advertise their movements—especially when they're travelling in Europe, say, or the Far East. That's why, if I decide we need a representative of the press at the meeting, he—or she'—Steiner smiled pleasantly—'would have to accept cheerfully some restriction on his or her own movements. And of course on what he or she wrote.'

'I understand. Of course!' She was all eagerness. 'Gosh, Mr Steiner, are you telling me what I think you're telling me? That you are accrediting me as a press representative at the meeting?'

Steiner offered her a cigarette, which she refused, and took one himself. 'The Senator told you where the meeting is to be?'

'No, I don't believe he knows himself. It's all rather mysterious.'

This was true. The usual practice, in advance of every previous meeting, had been for him to communicate the location, two weeks in advance, to the State Department —who of course passed the information on to the C.I.A. Routine. Everything open and above-board. A cultural get-together with distinguished patronage. Harmless!

Actually, espionage and conspiracy, with an official rubber stamp!

130

This year the meeting would be very special and unusual. Perhaps the last before millions who hadn't stopped worrying and loved the bomb would be dead. Certain arrangements had already been made with an air charter company whose chief executive, a man of Turkish origin with an Austrian passport, was one of Steiner's most trusted lieutenants.

Steiner modulated the friendly welcome-to-the-Senator's-niece smile to a look of gravity. 'This work,' he said, very seriously, 'demands more than dedication to a job. It demands a deep understanding. A deep humility. Fundamentally it is work for the same principle on which our country was founded: the right of every man to freedom.'

He had spoken the words many times before, at women's clubs all over America. By now the catch in his voice, histrionically most affecting, was automatic.

'Oh, I understand. I really do!' The catch in Anna's voice was equally effective.

Steiner got up. 'Nice meeting you, Miss O'Connor. Keep in touch!'

After Anna had left, Steiner spent a few moments in profound thought, then picked up the phone.

A voice said, 'Hugo!'

For a moment, Steiner listened to the somewhat stertorous breathing at the other end. Then he said, teasingly, 'You should lose some weight, Hugo. All that beer, all that *Leberknödel Suppe!* It's bad for you.'

'I know it,' Hugo said, in German. 'But without beer and food what is there?'

'Women,' Steiner replied, succinctly. 'I'll need the car. In half an hour.'

Steiner regularly searched his own apartment for hidden microphones and so far had found nothing. Still, it was impossible to be too careful. The car was the only place he was sure wasn't bugged.

Chapter Fourteen

New town, strange town. No friends. What does the visiting spy do? Anna lay on her bed in Room 222 at the Intercontinental and pondered the problem. She had been to the cinema three times in three days, seen one bad German film, a bit of *cinéma vérité* nonsense from France, and an American movie about sin and sex in Los Angeles, silly story with one redeeming feature. Wonderful shots of the Pacific ocean pounding the Californian shore. You could almost smell the sea, as well as hear it on the sound track. It brought the indolent sand-lizard out in her. Back in the hotel capsule, she thought this was no place to be in the summer.

There was a radio in the room, TV, ice-water; soothing décor, air-conditioning and double windows that shut out the city sounds from way down below. She might have been suspended from a balloon—lost in a cave under the Pyrenees.

The isolation, the loneliness of commercial travellers, men who have left their wives (or vice versa)—and spies.

The TV played the Beatles, the radio played Bach. She switched both off, kicked off her shoes and lay down on the bed with a Scotch—the last drop of duty free.

Duty free? Suddenly she could almost feel Sarratt's eyes

watching her, and, incidentally, bringing out the goose pimples. Now if he were in the room—and willing. . . . She reached out for the phone and gave the operator the number.

'Steiner.'

'Hi,' she said, cutely, 'it's me, still keeping in touch.'

'Well, hello, Miss O'Connor! Nice to hear from you.'

Both had used practically the same phrases on the two previous evenings when she had called. It was getting monotonous.

He said, 'I really do owe you an apology, Miss O'Connor. I naturally intended to invite you to dinner, but I've been so tied up . . .'

'Oh, I understand. You're a very busy, important man.'

She had guessed he liked to be buttered up. 'I just want to be sure you don't leave town and forget all about me.'

'No chance of that, Miss O'Connor. You've no friends, young people of your own age, in town?'

Anna said no, unfortunately, she hadn't. She also said she wasn't too sure about European dating habits, and uncle had told her to be careful.

Steiner said that uncle was one hundred per cent right. However, all European men weren't wolves. Would she care to come to a cocktail party he was giving the following evening? Say around six. She would! Well, that was fine.

Anna hung up. His manner was perfect. A middle-aged American egg-head gallantly doing the honours for a young, attractive and influential visiting fellow country-woman. A comfortably married man fulfilling a social and professional obligation.

Why then did the hotel room, oppressive, claustrophobic five minutes ago, now seem snug, safe? And if so, why did her flesh creep?

Steiner was taking another drive, north-east along the *Autobahn* towards Bad Nauheim. Hugo drove the Mercedes

133

220 SE with ruthless skill, immovable in the outer lane, the speedometer equally immovable on 90 miles, 144.83 k.p.h. He swooped down on a Volks 1500, a Fiat 1100 and a British MG, brushing them aside like flies. But through the rear mirror Hugo could see something coming up fast—a Jaguar.

With the next long down-grade, Hugo gave the Mercedes maximum throttle. The speedometer went up to 105 m.p.h. So much, no more. As the road levelled out, it sank back to 100—flat out, still smooth, seemingly effortless, but with nothing more to come. The Jaguar flashed its headlights and as Hugo reluctantly pulled over, swept past.

Hugo slouched behind the wheel, nothing about him alert, apart from his eyes. He swung back, into the outer lane and watched the rapidly vanishing tail of the Jag.

He said in German, 'You get the message, Herr Steiner? There are a dozen cars, maybe more, that can show us a clean pair of heels. What about a Ford Galaxie?'

'Too ostentatious,' Steiner said.

'No! The natural thing to buy! American should buy American.' Hugo passed his tongue over his lips and prepared to do battle with an Alfa Romeo Guilia. It was neck and neck.

'Something with plenty of power,' he said. 'No messing about.' He managed to crowd the Alfa behind a truck and got past. He said, 'Maybe there'll come a time when we'll really need that extra power.'

Steiner sat back and watched the road unravelling in front of them. He didn't go for a drive with Hugo simply for privacy, because the car wasn't bugged. Sitting beside Hugo on the *Autobahn* was an aesthetic experience. Once Hugo had been a racing driver, and it showed in everything he did on the road. It wasn't simply that he anticipated what was around every corner. He knew, positively, exactly, what every driver ahead was going to do. One glance at the way a man sat at the wheel, the smallest gesture, the line he took

134

through a bend was enough. Hugo had him taped. As a physician of genius can usually tell much of what he needs to know about a patient merely by looking at him, so for Hugo just watching the way the driver in front behaved for a few seconds was enough. This gave him astonishing anticipation of every hazard. Traffic ahead simply melted away. It was uncanny.

Hugo was also a good judge of a certain type of men, and he formed his opinion by going for a drive with them—letting them drive him. Not a scientific method of assessment, perhaps. But Hugo would say, 'Anything you can't learn about a man on the *Autobahn* between Frankfurt and Karlsruhe isn't worth knowing.'

What did such a drive show on that dangerous stretch of road, in Europe second for accidents, perhaps, only to France's R.N.7? It showed a man's courage, his judgment, his discretion, his degree of sheer ruthlessness, his willingness to take calculated risks.

Especially as Hugo invariably insisted that the test should be completed at an *average* speed of 80 m.p.h. Steiner relied on Hugo's judgment and did not give assignments to members of his A and T Squad (meaning Assassination and Terror) unless Hugo had pronounced them okay.

An exception had been Hagmann. Hugo, after doing the Frankfurt-Karlsruhe stretch with Hagmann twice, as a reassessment exercise, had decided he had become an unstable, inconsistent character, unpredictable and therefore potentially dangerous.

Hagmann had, however, other qualities of which Hugo was unaware—such as a formidable record in the S.S.—which had decided Steiner in his favour.

Who had been right? The issue, it seemed, would now never be settled.

Steiner watched, fascinated, as Hugo overtook a whole string of at least a dozen other vehicles, his headlights flashing, pinning them in the nearside lane, helpless to overtake each other, by the sheer speed and implacable inevitability of his approach.

He said, 'You've selected the right man for this particular job?'

'Don't worry. She's coming to your party?'

Steiner nodded. 'This particular job may be insignificant. On the other hand it may be vital for all of us, the whole Organization. It's important, therefore, that the operative should find out the truth about this girl and act on his findings, if unfavourable, without delay.'

When giving a subordinate instructions or discussing action to be taken, Steiner was apt to sound as if he were dictating a memorandum.

Hugo, from force of habit and example, responded in similar manner.

'Noted,' he said. 'The operative selected has been fully briefed. In background, speech, appearance, and apparent character, he's the best available man for the job. To deal with this particular girl.'

'I'm relying on your decision.'

Hugo said, 'You won't be disappointed.'

'I hope I won't be disappointed with the way things go in Rangoon, either. What's the time differential?'

'Seven and a half hours plus.'

Steiner glanced at his watch. It showed twelve-thirty. Seven-thirty p.m. in Rangoon, on the other side of the world.

Deadline. Curtains for the General.

The Bad Nauheim sign came up. Three miles.

'The usual place for lunch,' Steiner said. Hugo licked his lips and looked almost animated. Food was his life. And indeed, in a very real sense, he owed his life to food. His doctor said, tipping the scales at more than fourteen stone, his eating habits were endangering his life. Hugo knew better.

His great weight had slowed him down, made him chairborne, promoted him from operational to executive status.

136

And that was healthy. Hugo knew that in five years, out of a dozen highly-trained operatives in the A and T Squad only one had survived death either at the hands of a prospective victim, a secret service man, or another member of the Squad. The name of that man was Hugo!

Now Hugo swallowed his saliva, thought about eel soup and *Holsteiner Schnitzel*. Perhaps a portion of *Spätzle* to follow.

All fat men should live for ever. Idly Hugo wondered if the General was a fat man.

The General was, in fact, slightly less trim of figure than usual. This was because under his shirt he was wearing a bullet-proof vest. A longish garment extending from neck to groin, a new type, recently developed in the U.S. It afforded a high degree of protection against revolver bullets of all the usual calibre fired at close range. Such a bullet might break a rib, badly lacerate the skin and provoke much pain. It would be unlikely to kill. It also gave protection against knife or dagger.

Against high velocity rifles and bombs, it was useless.

The General, on instructions from Sarratt and Garris, had been wearing the vest since rising shortly after seven, and now, in the evening, he was beginning to feel damnably hot and uncomfortable.

Also on instructions, he had spent the day exactly according to schedule. From breakfast till lunch working at his office in the villa. There he received two or three official visitors—an aide to the Foreign Minister, the British Chargé d'Affaires, and a visiting American businessman—all unlikely assassins. Still, the General wore his vest.

Lunch he took alone, had his siesta in a different room from usual, just to be on the safe side; and composed himself for what the secret service men thought would be the real time of danger, the evening. In particular the reception in his honour at the American Embassy, announced months ago, and which supplied the reason why he was a marked man. The assassin knew exactly where he would be—and could make plans accordingly.

After his siesta, the General took a shower, not forgetting to take his bullet-proof vest with him into the bathroom. There he put on his dress trousers, white silk tuxedo. With his decorations, trim figure and general air of military man of distinction, he was still an imposing, handsome figure. Washington hostesses adored him, and with reason. Old soldiers don't die, he thought, they go to cocktail parties.

And now, in a drawing-room of all places, at a reception in his honour, he was facing death, the last enemy. Ironic!

At the elaborate buffet, he ate sparingly, partly because he was careful about his weight, partly because there was a chance that any special dish offered might be poisoned.

The General had talked to perhaps fifty people of two dozen nationalities. It was nine-thirty and he was still waiting to be shot, stabbed or otherwise disposed of. He was not frightened, merely irritated at being kept waiting.

He had taken only a little Scotch on the rocks. His role was to hold the assassin, once revealed, and it was vital to keep his wits about him.

Now, as he listened to a pretty Indian woman talking far too knowledgeably for him to follow about Bernard Buffet, he looked over the sea of faces, white, pink, yellow, of the people who had come to honour him.

Why? Because they were in the diplomatic service and it was their job? Because they were flattered to be invited to the Embassy? Because they wanted a free drink? And, if you could believe the secret service men, there was one guest whose sole purpose in coming was to kill him.

The General almost liked the unknown assassin. About him, at least, there was nothing phoney.

In two different parts of the salon, he saw the Limey, Sarratt, and Garris. The British Ambassador had introduced

138

Sarratt, the U.S. Ambassador had introduced Garris. He had greeted both as if meeting them for the first time.

Among the guests, the General was aware, there were several so-called intellectuals, egg-heads. A British writer, mugging up the Far East for his next book; an American professor (born Dresden, now a citizen, subject physics), and a party of mid-Europeans—a poet, a painter, a novelist, and a musician—who were on a world tour, all expenses paid, to tell the enslaved peoples everywhere how much better things were in the West. And they should know! There was also a British M.P. and his wife who, by judicious membership of the right committees with international connexions hadn't laid out hard cash for a holiday in the last ten years.

Frankly, if this was a battlefield, the General preferred the Normandy beaches. Why the hell hadn't the President allowed him to retire!

The Indian woman, sensing his indifference to Buffet, had slipped away.

'Good evening, General! Many, many happy returns!'

This time his tormentor was the First Secretary's wife. He grinned his displeasure, spent a few minutes in fatuous small-talk, then escaped to the john.

Being an American john it was of course civilized, deodorized, sterile, inorganic as a morgue. The General doused his face in cold water, aware that the man at the next basin was Garris. Good man, Garris, faithful even to the john. Just the two of them. The protector and the protected, peeing and washing together. Poetic.

The doors to the two W.C.s were open, so they were alone. The General, therefore, thought it safe to speak.

He said, drying his face on a spotless towel, 'Nine-thirty! Just two and a half hours to go! Say, maybe you got this whole thing wrong.'

'Maybe.'

In spite of the air conditioning, it was still unbearably hot.

The General found a bottle of cologne and, his eyes closed, dabbed his face with it.

His eyes being closed, he did not see the man who came in. It was in fact the mid-European pianist whose astonishingly rapid finger-work had been enthused over by the music critics of five continents.

This pianist had escaped to the West in 1956, was the friend of diplomats, scientists, industrialists. He played brilliant tennis, owned a Maserati, which he drove to engagements all over Europe with controlled brilliance. The quality of his driving was also the quality of his musicianship. Astonishing physical dexterity—but cold, uncommitted.

A critic had once written: 'Every effect calculated to the ultimate degree, implacable, infallible—and ultimately, after our initial astonishment, unbearable. Here, indeed, is the computer of the keyboard!'

In spite of such perceptive stuff, he was lionized in the West, especially in America. Anyway, the critic, threatened with libel, had been forced to resign, apologize, and was now teaching the piano, which he did badly, to children in Kansas.

Garris, knowing the pianist was a good, sound, our-side fellow, grinned at him in friendly fashion as he came into the john.

The pianist grinned back, also in friendly fashion, and shot Garris, with a silenced revolver of Italian manufacture, in the heart.

Then, with the manual dexterity for which he was famous, he shot at the General's heart, too.

The General looked at him, astonished. He had been introduced to the fellow not an hour ago. In spite of all the preliminary briefing, what was happening now just seemed intolerably bad manners. Like being shot at, after a declared truce, on Christmas Day. Shot by the pianist! A ridiculous switch on the old joke.

There was an intolerable pain over his heart. But the General had been wounded before. Wounded, he had performed deeds of great and simple courage.

Now he lunged towards the musician who stepped back, a puzzled expression on his face. A man shot to the heart should fall dead.

When the General failed to fall dead, the musician realized, in a flash, there had to be a reason. Nothing psychological or magical, but strictly physical. If a man shot to the heart remained standing, that could only mean something stood between the heart and the bullet.

He fired the third bullet at the General's face. This time there was no doubt. The face which, a split second before, had been smooth, dried by the astringent cologne, was suddenly an obscene, stricken, blood-stained mask of horror.

And the General, good soldier to the last, fell without so much as an oath, to the tiled and clinical coolness of the john's floor, where his blood made an unseemly pattern.

Faintly, from the salon, the pianist heard the sound of the Mozart aria. 'Alleluia . . . alleluia. . . .' Pure, clear notes of infinite innocence. The Chinese soprano from Formosa sang the Texan General to eternal rest.

The pianist did not pause to reflect on the significance, if any, of this. He tossed the gun out of the window of one of the W.C.s to lend colour to the idea that the assassin had dropped it in flight.

He then slipped out of the john, glided down an empty corridor to the room which had been allotted to him for relaxation before his performance.

'Alleluia . . . alleluia. . . .' From the salon, the notes still came, serene and pure, like a benediction. He peeled off his white cotton gloves, took a drink of imported mineral water, then lay on the chaise longue.

His pulse was normal, his breathing steady. His eye fell on the clock. He had been out of the room for rather less than three minutes. He closed his eyes.

141

The Mozart died away in quiet ecstasy. Applause, and a tap on the door. The pianist looked at the native servant like a man awakened from sleep.

A few moments later, after his hostess's gushing introduction, he seated himself at the Steinway, an impressive figure, head bowed, in concentration of will.

Then, as if in a trance, his hands, long, beautiful, demonic, actuated by some invisible power, began their manipulation of the keyboard.

Hypnotized, his audience received his interpretation of the *Italian Concerto*. The hostess glanced round, looking for the guest of honour. But it was a large room, with many columns and luxuriant plants. It was impossible to say whether he was present or not.

Sarratt, fascinated by the music, *knew* that the General was not present. He also knew that the General's idea of music was *South Pacific*, and that Bach made him squirm. He was also aware that Garris was not present either.

So all would be well.

It was exactly nine-thirty p.m., local time.

Two-thirty in Germany. Steiner and Hugo climbed back into the Mercedes, this time Steiner at the wheel. Purely a safety precaution, since Hugo was filled with food and drink. Hugo always conducted his 'tests' on an empty stomach.

Steiner turned on the radio, ready for a news broadcast.

'It's too early,' Hugo said. He settled down in his seat, reached for a tablet to settle his stomach—that second portion of dumpling had been just à little too much—and closed his eyes. 'Give them a couple of hours. They'll have to consult Washington, decide on a story . . .' He belched quietly. 'These things take time.' He sounded bored.

Chapter Fifteen

Anna arrived for the party in a cute black dress, smelling sweet and cool, exuding girlish enthusiasm.

'Let me introduce Miss Anna O'Connor . . . the Senator's niece . . . helping with public relations . . .'

On such occasions, Steiner missed Mrs Steiner. Her social gush came more readily than his. The usual kind of crowd. A mixed bunch of intellectuals, vociferously anti-Commie.

Steiner smiled at them, felt contempt. If they had four legs they would sit up and beg, if not for a trip to the United States or Britain, then for a cocktail canape, a dry martini, or a pack of Pall Mall. Steiner the circus master, practitioner of the conditioned reflex.

Steiner looked around the room, smiling benevolently. Who was that guy with Anna O'Connor? A friend of Hugo's without doubt! *The* friend?

Steiner watched, listened to, even sniffed the stranger with interest.

Dark, svelt, immaculately tailored, discreet cologne. *Simpatico. Molto.*

Grudgingly Steiner felt admiration for Hugo's judgment. The girl was obviously attracted, receiving the Grade A treatment: eyes only for you, where've you been all my life, the full come-to-Italy-and-love routine.

Steiner watched, fascinated, listening politely meanwhile as a Rumanian journalist, between sips of dry martini, described to him the horrors of a Bucharest jail he knew nothing of at first hand. One of the more amateurish potential spies.

Steiner simulated interest, talked of possible lecture tours in America, Japan. A useful man for small-time stuff perhaps, but too obvious, too anxiously on-the-make. The profession was becoming too damned attractive, too many jobs chasing too many men and women, usually of the wrong type. They would be forming a spies union next, claiming minimum rates, unemployment benefit, pensions, and affiliation to the C.I.O. and the T.U.C. They would even start putting in a man's passport: profession—spy!

This girl Anna O'Connor. So she looked like a co-ed! So did many of the most successful whores! So what! It could mean everything, or nothing.

Steiner switched his attention from the Rumanian to a Latvian sculptor and his wife who had just arrived, then to an English professor, and wife, who was giving a series of lectures at West German universities, all expenses paid, naturally. Guests arrived every moment. Steiner was much occupied with greeting people, seeing that they had drinks.

When next he looked towards Anna O'Connor there were three people around her. Gino, the *simpatico* Italian, a woman named Gerda whom Steiner had once tried to seduce and whom he knew to be queer, and a young American— glasses, tweed suit, vague academic manner, freckles.

Steiner remembered Hugo saying something about hedging his bets. Which was sensible. There was no guarantee that Anna would conveniently pair up with the first man of Hugo's choice. There was no accounting for taste. And, frankly, it hadn't occurred to him that the girl might be like *that*. If so Gerda would be able to cope!

Steiner began to edge closer to the little group, but the

room was packed now. A Bulgarian poet of immense girth and volubility cornered him. When he looked again the group had broken up. Anna and the Italian had disappeared. Gerda and the American were leaving, together.

None of them had said good-bye. It was that kind of party.

Steiner took another tomato juice and for the moment put Anna out of his mind. These parties were important, an essential part of the front. Several people present were firmly convinced the Organization was a great power for good, and supported it with hard cash. To them Steiner was a dedicated man, a prophet. He had to act the part, though by this time acting hardly entered into it. The role had become second nature.

Eyes half closed, as if in prayer, Steiner launched into a dissertation on the function of the *émigré* writer and artist as instruments of international good will, as valuable counters in the never-ending war against Communism.

The hopeful gathered round expectantly, wondering on whom the prophet, when he opened his eyes, would look with favour. Many were called, few chosen. . . .

Gino owned a red Alfa roadster which he drove with insolent panache through the city, into the country. He had not told her, and she had not asked, where they were going. Since leaving Steiner's apartment, neither had spoken a word. She had simply been glad to get away from the young tweedy American and Gerda. Both of them, it seemed, were checking up on her, filing away in their minds her every word and gesture.

Gino was equally suspect, naturally. But at least with him there was a strong physical attraction, immediate, chemical. Discovering just what he wanted from her should, at least, be interesting. Anyway, it was, she told herself, her duty as an agent to lead him on. Sarratt would approve.

Anna relaxed, waited. A few kilometres before Geinhausen, the Alfa turned off down a minor road, rutted, partly covered with grass. The trees closed in and then, suddenly, the car swung under an archway. They were in the Middle Ages.

The *Schloss* was built round a central courtyard. External staircases led to the upper floors. Gino swung the car into what had once been the coach-house and cut the engine. The silence became tangible.

Anna got out of the car, walked to the centre of the courtyard.

Still neither spoke. In the half-light Anna looked from window to window. All were closed and grimy, a few broken. No smoke from the chimneys, no voices, no sign of human habitation. The place had the feel of not having been lived in for a hundred years—and also the indefinable feel of evil.

Anna's inspection came full circle and finished on Gino, the object, as they say, of the exercise. Their eyes met, his showing nothing but what she expected. He turned, walked to the nearest staircase, leaving her to follow.

The lock, Anna saw at once, was modern. Of course Gino had a key. He stood aside politely, inviting her to enter first.

An unexpected room. Chintz-covered chairs, a record-player—battery-operated transistor, Anna surmised at once, since candles seemed to provide the only source of illumination. A table with drinks—gin, whisky, champagne—and heavy crystal glasses. The room was free of dust, she also noted, which argued fairly regular occupation.

Headquarters, hide-out, love-nest? Why oddly familiar?

Gino closed the door, moved to the drinks table. He picked up a champagne bottle and glanced at her. She nodded.

The champagne was not cold enough, of course, but very good nevertheless. The first she'd had since the studio. And with the first sip, she knew why the place was familiar. Like

146

the room at the studio, it was another testing place, an arena. Sarratt, the English operator, had denied her the ultimate test of insincerity between man and woman. Disappointingly.

Of this one's intentions she had no doubt at all.

Pouring the champagne, he had also started the music. Liszt, the *Fountains at the Villa d'Este*, limpid, hypnotic, each note separate as a drop of water, yet forming a continuous, glittering, magic stream.

He must have been watching her through the mirror above the mantelpiece, because he said—almost the first words since leaving the party—'You know the record?'

She nodded. 'Cziffra.'

It did not occur to her then that she had pronounced the artist's name correctly, as a Hungarian would. He came close to her and untied the silk headscarf she had worn in the car. As he did so, he kissed her forehead, almost respectfully, as if she were some kind of idol or relic. And it did not occur to her either that, besides kissing her forehead, he was examining the roots of her hair to discover whether it was tinted, and if so what the original colour could be.

Anna was, frankly, too hungry for his body to care. She waited, rapt, eyes closed, flowering to him, as he undid the zip of her dress. Her arms about his neck, eyes still closed, he lifted her from the small circle of silk at her ankles and carried her to the bed.

Only too late in the love-making did she realize it was not a seduction but an investigation. A vivisection. Operated upon, she was supposed to yield her essential self to patient, dedicated, infinitely skilled—but in the last resort—utterly passionless—analysis.

This was not a bed, but a laboratory. Her every movement, her slightest sound a matter for cold-blooded conjecture.

Ultimately, he had his reward, at the moment of great pleasure.

147

Two little words. '*Jaj! Istenem!*' The all-purpose word in Hungarian. The alpha and the omega. The cry of grief, of pain, of pleasure. A cry linking man and woman *in extremis*, with good and evil, with God and the devil.

Gino rose from his investigation, placed two cigarettes in his mouth, lit them, then placed one between her lips. *Cliché!*

It was the first cigarette she had smoked for several months. It tasted rough, acrid, almost asphyxiating. She took it from between her lips and held it between her fingers, watching him. He poured two glasses of champagne, handed her one, raised his, as if in toast, and drank it at a gulp, watching her in the mirror.

Anna returned the interest. Gino was lean, muscular, but not muscle-bound, an almost perfect instrument. She had often, but not always, been able to dissociate herself from physical pleasure. Till now she had always taken a man when he pleased her, when she wanted him, assessing him, in terms of pleasure. Sexually, it was essential, if he were to mean anything, that he should be *soigné, copieux*, and, above all, provide the ambiance that was essential to raise sexual union to something emotionally satisfying instead of mere rutting. Bedding, in fact, to her was rather like eating— according to one's built-in, innate code Michelin.

Till now the code had never misled her. Some feasts, of course, had been more satisfying than others. But always she had been fed, emotionally as well as physically.

Now, for the first time, investigated, examined, manipulated, she felt soiled. Like a whore. Was this the usual reaction of the female spy, she wondered, to the use of sex as just another useful piece of apparatus in the game, another gimmick?

Looking at the opposition, it occurred to her that he looked jaded, tired, even bored, like a gigolo at the end of the Roman tourist season. A spent gladiator of the Via Veneto.

148

Anna reached for her clothes, now strewn at the foot of the bed.

He was too quick for her, snatching them aside. Then he said, simply, 'Magyar!' He said it like a man announcing the solution of a riddle. Drawing on his vast experience of hundreds of women, his built-in computer coming up with the right answer with electronic accuracy.

He then took her arm, glanced at her right shoulder, said. 'The real Anna O'Connor, the Senator's niece, has a birthmark—just there!' He almost, but not quite, touched her skin with the tip of his burning cigarette. Anna shrank away.

Suddenly the opposition didn't look tired and jaded any more. He looked more interested and excited than during the love-making. Anna thought of Sarratt saying, during her initiation, 'You'll find yourself in spots directly attributable to me—my orders. And you'll damn me to hell!'

The odd thing was that she didn't feel like damning Sarratt, just anxious not to let him down. Not letting him down! Those were the exact words, unspoken, that came to her. The opposition had called her 'Magyar', 'Hungarian', which, in a sense, was true enough. But not the whole truth. How much of her was English, American?

Gino sat down languidly, poured himself another glass of champagne. He said, conversationally, 'This place has an interesting history—especially the torture chamber in the cellars. Some of the equipment is medieval, some up to date. Say around 1945.'

'As used by the Nazis?'

'On some of their special victims. Partly to obtain information, partly for amusement.'

'And which is your special interest?'

'Both. Of course you've already revealed you're not the person you pretend to be. But a lot more could be obtained by the application of pleasurable—to me, at least—persuasion.

You would find it very painful. Frankly, I'd like that. Of course you could tell me now, right away, who you are, who you're working for, what precisely you hope to achieve by masquerading as the Senator's niece. But, frankly, I think your answers would be far more interesting—and truthful—down there.'

Anna thought quickly. Bluff was obviously useless. There remained two ways of dealing with him. She resolved to use, if necessary, both.

She said, in her best American accent, 'Of course you could be making a mistake. And if so. . . .' She drew her fingers over her throat.

'Magyar!' he said again. 'The real Anna O'Connor does not dye her hair. She has a birthmark on her right shoulder —and speaks only a little schoolgirl French. Hardly a word of any other language.'

Anna was about to say something, but he wagged a finger, admonishingly. 'Don't deny it, please. We have reliable sources of information in America. In particular, one girl who shared a room at Bryn Mawr with the real Anna O' Connor for a whole term.'

He watched her lazily, half smiling.

Possibly he was bluffing. More likely, he was not. But one thing was certain. Only he, at this moment, knew for certain that she was not the Senator's niece.

Anna made up her mind. 'All right,' she said, and smiled. 'So my name is not O'Connor and my grandfather did not come from Ireland, and I am not the Senator's niece. How much does Steiner pay you? A few hundred marks a month? I imagine your particular services aren't worth much more. You're crude, not very subtle as a lover, and personally, I don't care for obvious perfume on a man. I suppose you have your minor uses. To an ageing, and not very discriminating matron.'

His cheek twitched spasmodically as if she had struck him.

Anna smiled, now strangely relaxed. 'Name your price, Gino.'

'No,' he said. 'It's not that I don't like money, you understand. Simply that the people I work for don't let their employees resign.'

'Why resign? Just take on a little discreet, part-time extra work. Who's to know but us? Cosy, convenient and rewarding.'

For a fraction of a second indecision clouded his eyes.

He said then, 'I'm not afraid to take reasonable risks. But what you suggest is too dangerous.'

'Pity. Personally, I'd do almost anything for money.'

'Meaning you'd like to work for us? Part-time?'

'Why not? I like to live well, I have expensive tastes.'

He said, 'It is, perhaps, something we could discuss—when you have told me everything.' He got up and moved towards her. 'I'll show you the basement.'

His arm shot out and he grabbed her right wrist. A second later, he had twisted her arm behind her back and jerked her off the bed in a single movement.

A spiral staircase, black as the tomb, dank and evil-smelling. Every now and then his knee gave her a little push in the small of her back to keep her moving. Down . . . down . . . perhaps fifty feet.

Then no more stairs, the floor suddenly flat. She could hear him moving very quietly a yard or so away, but the blackness was total. Anna shivered, her teeth chattering. But she felt now not terrified so much as inexplicably excited. Just as she had before being subjected to the torments back at the base in Kent. Once she had had a boy friend in the Marines who told her the training was so tough, even brutal, that when he went into action for the first time, it seemed almost an anti-climax, a piece of cake.

Was that how she felt now? Was this really *it*—a dank, smelly medieval torture chamber presided over by a sadistic *pappagallo* who smelled too strongly of cologne?

151

A light suddenly blinded her, a spotlight that picked her out as if she were on stage.

Gino must have been standing behind it. He was quite invisible.

'Now, please look around,' he said in the tone of a smooth, practised guide showing off the most precious treasures of a great house.

The spotlight moved away from her smoothly and picked out a mummy-like object against one of the sweating walls.

'The iron maiden,' the guide remarked. 'The victim is placed inside, screws are tightened, knives of various lengths pierce the flesh. One knife points directly at the heart. An interesting contrivance but it doesn't amuse me especially. It is difficult to enjoy the sufferings of the victim.'

The spotlight moved on, pinpointing a thumb-screw, the water-torture—then, appallingly, three half-starved rats in a cage. 'I don't think we'll concern ourselves with them,' Gino said. 'I'm rather fastidious, personally, and messing about with rats would torture me almost as much as it would you.'

Anna noted the 'messing about'. Gino's English was remarkably idiomatic. An English education? Eton and Christ Church? 'You've thought about a career, my boy? The army, commerce, science, the diplomatic service?' 'Well, actually, no, sir. I rather thought I'd have a shot at seducing, and ultimately torturing women. You know, real postgraduate stuff.' Anna giggled, inwardly.

Or did the idioms simply indicate a long, long misspent youth pandering to how many scores, hundreds of lonely, hungry, hopeful, pathetic Englishwomen cast up like flotsam against the pavements of Rome?

'Oh, in case you're wondering,' Gino said, 'this spotlight works off a car battery. If we *did* have electricity, at the right voltage, all sorts of pleasures would be possible. Unfortunately . . .'

The spotlight moved abruptly to a grating in the floor of the chamber.

'*Ecco!*' Gino said. 'Go to the grating—and listen.'

Anna moved as she was bidden.

'Listen!' he said again.

In the silence, at a great distance, a faint rushing sound. Like the wind in the trees, or a waterfall, infinitely remote.

'You hear?'

'Yes.'

'The *Schloss* was built on this particular spot in the fifteenth century,' Gino continued in his best guide's voice, 'not because the site had any particular strategic value or scenic charm. But merely because the margrave, who was a man of strange and compulsive vices, heard that sound. The sound, of course, of underground waters. Men have been lowered at the end of ropes. The longest descent, I think, was a thousand feet, sometime in the 'thirties of this century. Something went wrong with the winch, and the poor fellow was hanging at the end of the rope for about an hour. His light failed. When at last he was hauled to the surface, unfortunately he couldn't tell anything to anybody about his experience because he was just an incoherent, babbling, human wreck. He died, years later, in a lunatic asylum. Some say the margrave used the cavern as a huge underground graveyard for his innumerable victims—a kind of subterranean Bosporus that conceals thousands and thousands of bodies. Some say it's inhabited by a race of submen. Some say it's the entrance to hell. And some say Hitler escaped from the bunker and went to live there . . .'

Suddenly Gino materialized, emerging from behind the lamp. There was a click as he used his lighter to start a cigarette. He came over to her. 'But why speculate about the secrets of the place when, unless you are a very good and truthful girl, you will discover them for yourself!'

He came still closer, and Anna saw that he held a length of cord. 'Hold out your hands.'

'Try and make me!'

153

Gino's hand flashed out, Anna stepped aside and put out her foot. He tripped, staggered, but recovered his balance.

The cigarette he had just lit was on the floor. Anna ducked, picked it up and thrust it against his face. He howled with pain and swore in an operatic-like recitative in Italian.

'*Bene!*' he said then. 'Now we stop playing games.'

From his hip he took a short rubber truncheon, looped the cord round his wrist. Then he came at her again, driving her back against the wall. Her knee came up to kick him in the stomach, but a little slow. The truncheon crashed against the side of her head.

Throbbing blackness, through which shooting stars flashed, exploded.

She was dimly aware of a smell—cologne—and then another, even more pungent, that filled her mouth and nose suffocatingly. She struggled, fought against it, gasping for breath. Then she went limp. . . .

Was it five minutes, ten, before consciousness returned? First she was aware only of the abominable pain in her head. Then she realized she was in a still greater pain, a pain that started with her wrists, extending to the arms and shoulders. As if every joint were being pulled apart by the entire weight of her body. . . .

She looked up and became aware, as the chloroform-induced fog over her brain lifted, that that was exactly what *was* happening.

Her wrists were tied together, and from them a rope passed over a beam a few feet above. Suspended, her body swayed to and fro, gently, lazily, like a pendulum. Tick . . . tock . . . Anna's become a clock!

She looked down, down the gleaming length of her body, and saw something else. She was ticking away directly over the grating that covered the pit.

Gino was directly below her. The grating seemed to be stuck. He gasped and grunted as he struggled with it.

Anna looked up again, and her eyes, now accustomed to the glare, looked along the course of the rope that suspended her. It passed over the beam and was tied to an iron ring in the wall.

She made out a smaller brilliance. Close to the ring was a candle. The rope would burn through, slowly, giving her plenty of time to talk. And if she didn't, there was the pit below.

The oscillations of her body became smaller. She made no sound, feigning unconsciousness. Now and again Gino looked up at her, then again worked away, with a diligence his employers would have found commendable, at the grating.

A last effort and the pit yawned immediately beneath her, a great black mouth, ready to swallow.

Gino stretched his back, sighed, like a man relaxing after honest toil.

Anna kept her eyes half closed. He was looking up at her.

'Hey!' he said. 'Hey! *Bambina. Ciao!*'

He might have been on a Roman sidewalk.

'Hey! *Bambina!*'

This time he tickled the soles of her feet. She opened her eyes. He grinned, painfully, because his cheek had an ugly mark where she had stubbed the cigarette out on it.

'Look around, *bambina!*' he said. 'Look down at the pit, look at the rope that's holding you up. Look at the candle.'

He placed the candle about two feet below the rope. It would get hot, then smoulder, catch fire. . . . Anna shuddered.

The pain in her arms and shoulders was almost intolerable. How long could human muscle stand such strain before permanent damage. . . . Permanent! In ten minutes, she'd be in a huge, watery grave, thousands of feet deep.

She thought fleetingly of Sarratt. 'There'll be times when you'll damn me to hell!'

'Damn him!' she said. 'Damn him!'

155

'How's that again, *bellissima!* Damn who?'

She uttered a little scream. 'Let me down!'

'Talk first. Quickly! Look at the candle.'

The rope was beginning to smoulder, giving off its own smoke.

'I . . . I was sent to find out about Steiner. . . .'

'Yes, yes, but who sent you? What do they already know about Steiner? Or do they only suspect?'

Gino glanced at the candle. Would she talk quickly enough? To remove the candle and start all over again would waste valuable time. He decided to keep up the pressure.

'I don't want to die!' Anna screamed. 'I don't want to die!'

'Then talk, *bambina*, talk!'

'Yes, yes . . .' she gasped. 'I. . . .'

She let her head fall forward, forced herself to go limp.

Through half-closed eyes, she sensed rather than saw him coming close. Then, with a single convulsive movement, she raised her legs, and as in a vice, had him round the neck and shoulders. He was caught completely unawares, off-balance. Now he was clinging to her, suspended over the pit. But her body was wet with sweat. Anna looked at the candle. The rope was burning now. How long had she got, a minute, perhaps only seconds?

Gino clung to her like an ecstatic lover, sobbing. Then she could feel him slipping, almost imperceptibly. But slipping.

Her body bathed in sweat, it was this, the physical manifestation of her pain, her fear, her terror, that killed Gino.

For a few abject seconds he fought to hold on to her. They looked into each other's faces, only inches apart. His eyes looked into hers, for help, comfort, when no help or comfort were possible.

Then, quite suddenly, he was gone. There was a scream. A scream that shrilled and vanished.

156

Anna felt lonely. Curious, but true. If it had been within her power, she would have called him back.

There was a sudden jerk, and her body dropped about an inch. One strand of the rope had parted.

She began to bend her knees and kick . . . bend and kick. . . .

Slowly, slowly, the pendulum began again. Not to panic! Keep the movements even, rhythmical! The open hole was at least five feet wide. . . . Bend and kick . . . bend and kick. . . . The movement was oddly familiar, as if she were on a swing in a garden she had known as a child.

A game, she told herself. Don't panic.

She closed her eyes, forced herself to concentrate on the swinging movement. If the rope parted when she was over the abyss, then at least she would see nothing. Her arms and shoulders now were numb. Her brain reeled at the thought of approaching death, obliteration. Was this what it was like to be crucified? Oh, God! . . .

Suddenly, the tension in her arms vanished, and she felt herself falling . . . falling . . . interminable.

Face downwards, she hit the rock floor, ankles, knees, elbows all together with a sickening crack.

Only then did she open her eyes.

She raised her head, painfully. She was looking down, directly into the pit.

Shivering, whimpering with pain and relief, she pulled back from the abyss. Quietly, as if sliding into healing sleep, she passed out.

Chapter Sixteen

Crisis news in banner headlines, but the city crowds did not care. Theatres and cinemas were closing, cafés and night clubs filling up. The affluent milled along the pavements. Anna, telling the taxi driver to take her straight to the hotel, began to relax, to recall what had happened to her, almost as if the victim had been someone else. How, after recovering consciousness, she had managed to loosen the rope round her wrists with her teeth. The whole upper part of her body feeling permanently stretched, dislocated, yet still, somehow, she had managed to get the grating back over the abyss.

The spiral staircase, the bedroom again and a stiff drink, she had tidying the place up, wiping clear of prints everything she had touched. . . .

Then the courtyard, a great pool of shadows now, lit only by the faint glimmer of the stars.

The long moments of waiting, listening, watching. Surely there must be a caretaker, a watchman. But there was no light, no sound, nothing.

Almost invisible in her black dress, slipping from shadow to shadow till she came to the stable where Gino had left the Alfa. Groping through the darkness until at last she was behind the wheel, her fingers questing the knobs and switches like a blind person reading braille.

God! Suppose Gino had taken the ignition key with him down into hell!

She blamed herself for not memorizing the lay-out of the dashboard during the drive, made a mental note to be meticulous about such things in future. She turned a knob and a piercing wail assaulted the night air. The radio! A jazz clarinet. She killed it—then a second later found the ignition key—still in the dash. Gino had been foolish? Or just very cocky, utterly sure of himself?

Anna turned the key and the motor came to life. She stirred the gear-lever, looking for reverse, then gingerly backed out into the courtyard.

Without using the lights she edged the Alfa along the rough track through the woods. At the main road junction, she made absolutely sure no cars were coming, then turned on to the highway, pointing the car towards Frankfurt.

A few seconds later a black Mercedes came towards her. Hugo saw a red Alfa, and thought, 'So Gino has finished quickly. *Ein guter Kerl!* A swine! Where women are concerned—incomparable!'

Hugo thought of turning around and putting Gino to another little test—to check if his technique with the Alfa was as infallible as it was with women. But Hugo had eaten well, was feeling lazy, and the bed at the *Schloss* was comfortable. He might even spend the night there.

So Hugo's full belly was fortunate for Anna. Hugo drove on to the *Schloss*, Anna drove into the suburbs of Frankfurt.

She parked the car, circumspectly, outside a large block of flats. No need to worry about finger-prints now—she was wearing cotton gloves. Also a head scarf which made recognition difficult. She crossed the street, jumped on a bus, rode for a couple of kilometres, then took a taxi.

Apart from the excruciating pain in her arms, shoulder

and back, the ugly weals where the cord had bit into her wrists, a foul headache, and the knowledge that she had been possessed by a man she despised and hated—and who yet had pleasured her—the worst sensation, the worst pain of all—she felt fine.

The desk clerk gave her the key to her room without a second glance. But she felt as if sin, fornication, sudden death and espionage showed like the marks of plague. The blessed anonymity of hotels!

'Anna,' she said to herself going up in the elevator, 'Anna, what, in the name of all that's sacred, if *anything* is sacred, are you? What kind of doll?'

Doll! Tart! Broad! Take your pick.

In Room 222 she picked up the phone, asked for room service and whisky. A night for alcoholic, not barbiturate, oblivion.

She went into the bathroom, stripped off, put on a towelling dressing-gown. Suddenly, she felt all-in, but strangely happy. The impersonal hotel room, so much hated so short a time ago, was suddenly heaven. Where was Gino's body? Battered, floating in some infinitely vast, infinitely cold underground lake? She shuddered, pleasurably.

The waiter entered with a bottle of Scotch, a dish of ice.

He was good-looking, polite, correct, but with a slightly uncontrollable, roving eye. Also he seemed excited, wanted to talk.

'You are flying home, Fräulein?' His eye flickered to the open wardrobe. 'Not packed yet?'

He picked up the bottle, questioningly, from the tray.

'Open it,' she said. 'Why should I fly home?'

'Two months ago, I was released from the army. Tomorrow, next week, back again. What kind of luck would you call that in American?'

'Lousy.'

The waiter said, 'Most of the Americans have left already.'

'Well, I generally do the opposite of what most Americans do. I'm not a completely conditioned consumer.'

'Please? I don't understand.'

She said irritably. 'Look, bud, I'm in no mood for English lessons. Try Berlitz.'

He looked as if he were about to cry.

Anna relented. 'All right,' she said. 'Tell me about it. Tell me why all good Americans are flying home to Mom.'

So he told her about the assassination. About how the Americans suspected the Russians. How hysteria had gripped the entire Western world. How the President's finger was one-eighth of an inch above the button. The one that triggered the bomb.

'The Russians are moving troops through Poland towards the West,' the waiter added. 'Let me help you to pack, Fräulein. Anything can happen. The chef says we, the West Germans, ought to occupy East Germany right away. This, the chef says, is a great opportunity. Of course, the chef is mad.'

The waiter watched her like a man not expecting doom within twenty-four hours. As she walked about the room she had, perhaps, shown rather a lot of leg.

'At least, Fräulein,' he said very correctly, 'get dressed before the bomb falls.'

'If it's going to drop within a hundred miles of here, getting dressed hardly seems necessary,' Anna said. She gave him five marks. 'Thanks for the information and the advice.'

The waiter went out, puzzled, disappointed.

Anna sipped her whisky. So things were happening as Sarratt feared, as Hagmann said they would. Once again, the world was on the brink. Incredible, idiotic, true. Suppose the next assassination took place on schedule. What then?

Anna switched on the radio. 'The British,' the newscaster said, 'are urging moderation in Washington, and an early meeting of world leaders, somewhere on neutral ground.'

But what would the British be urging if a British cabinet minister, a well-known moderate, a neutralist, were the next to be knocked off?

Anna switched to another station. This time an Italian voice was recapping. The assassin had killed himself. Cyanide. In his death agony he had admitted that he was in the pay of the Russians. . . . Lies, Moscow had screamed, lies! The West had invented this *émigré* Bulgarian pianist assassin for their own wicked purposes. . . . This demented hireling, if he existed at all, was as much responsible as Van der Lubbe for the Reichstag fire. . . .

Anna switched off the hysteria, lay on the bed, sipped her whisky. Nervous and physical exhaustion set her hands shaking. Again. But slowly the whisky was soothing her down. She poured another shot. The last for the time being. It was necessary to remain sober, keep her wits about her.

Somewhere, far off, a bell was ringing. Fire-bell? Ambulance? She seemed to be falling through limitless blackness; a great rushing, as if an immense ocean were pouring over her, filled her ears. Gino fell past her, his face phosphorescent in the blackness. He grinned with black teeth, waved and disappeared. Still she fell, and still falling she saw herself, broken, on a rock. A great tide rushed over her, and she screamed, soundlessly, because her mouth, throat and lungs were filled with water, and all the time the bell rang. Panic-stricken, she fought against the water, vainly trying to reach the surface, arms and legs flailing. . . . Her arm struck something sharp and very solid, and she opened her eyes. . . .

The solid object was the bedside table, and the ringing came from the phone. Her eyes focused on her travelling clock. The hands pointed to nine. . . . She looked towards the window. Light seeped through the curtains. Nine a.m.!

Her limbs painfully stiff, she slid her legs off the bed, her toes hitting the empty whisky glass where it had fallen from her hand the night before when she had passed out.

The phone went on ringing, the sound boring intolerably into her brain. She picked up the instrument, less out of curiosity than to put an end to the torture.

'Anna?' Steiner's voice.

She answered with an unintelligible croak.

'Anna O'Connor? Who is this?' He sounded suspicious, edgy, disbelieving.

Anna forced herself into her role. Come misery, misfortune and migraine, the show must go on. 'You woke me up. Oh, thanks for the party. It was swell.' She took a gulp of water. 'I didn't expect to hear from you this morning, Mr Steiner.'

'Oh? Why not?'

Anna decided to play him a little. 'Not you. Not anybody.'

'I don't follow.'

'The war, Mr Steiner. The war.'

'Oh, that! The tension eased a bit overnight. Don't worry.' He sounded like a man with more important things to think about. He said, 'You left the party early. A date?'

'Ah ha.'

'What does that mean?'

'I don't care for one of your friends, Mr Steiner. Name of Gino. Martini, Martelli, something like that, vaguely alcoholic.' She yawned, and said, 'Sorry.'

There was a little silence while Steiner phrased his reply. He said, 'Gino's a nice boy. Good family, very well connected.'

'Well, he didn't connect with me. Not that he didn't try.'

'What happened?' Steiner sounded worried.

'One guess, Mr Steiner. He got fresh, and I said "goodnight" somewhere in the suburbs, just in time to catch a late movie.'

'Oh,' he sounded unconvinced. 'Well, that's disturbing.'

163

'Don't be disturbed, Mr Steiner. I won't tell uncle.' She laughed pleasantly.

Steiner laughed too, not so pleasantly. 'Well, you know, I do feel sort of responsible for you.'

'Oh, I'm a big girl now. Just don't invite him again.' There was silence while he thought that one over.

'Thanks for calling, Mr Steiner. I meant what I said about the party. Lovely! Now I'm going to order orange juice and coffee.'

'Anna!' He sounded urgent, like a man who's just made a snap decision.

'Yes, Mr Steiner?'

'Stick near the phone. There'll be an assignment for you. Something big.'

Steiner had made the call from a café. Hugo was waiting for him on the terrace, eating sausage, boiled eggs and rye bread like a starving man.

'She's back at the hotel,' Steiner said. 'She says Gino got fresh, and she left him, somewhere in the suburbs. You're sure you saw the car near the *Schloss?*'

'I saw a red Alfa. I didn't see the driver.'

'One thing's for sure. That Gino loused it up.'

'Gino doesn't make mistakes. Not where women are concerned.'

'Well, he made one this time. Also he didn't report, I want that guy's hide. Find him.'

'Maybe it's just as the girl said,' Hugo said, stuffing a piece of sausage into his mouth. 'She didn't fall for his sex appeal and that got him worried. Gino's a Sicilian. Sicilians take that sort of thing seriously. There's a first time for every man. It hurts.'

'You suggested we use him,' Steiner said. 'That makes you responsible.'

'I'll put another man on the job. Someone Nordic. Maybe she's allergic to Latins.'

164

'No,' Steiner said. 'There isn't time. She goes with us.'

'That wise?'

'We're afraid all of a sudden of a bit of a girl?'

'Women,' Hugo said, 'are always dangerous. If an expert like Gino fails . . .' He shrugged expressively. 'Watch out! You're not back to square one. You've learned a valuable lesson.'

'That,' said Steiner, 'is why she goes along.'

In Westminster the air was heavy with crisis. The police had sealed off Downing Street and the Parliament building. The house was sitting late. There were camp beds in many offices in the Ministry of Defence, and old hands talked of old times and 1939. But not, as Armageddon seemed close, nostalgically.

The Minister remained on the front bench till long after midnight. Then Sarratt saw him in his private room.

More than dangers to the state now weighed upon the Minister. Heavy-eyed, a film of perspiration covering his forehead, hand shaking as he reached for a cigarette, the Minister was afraid for his own skin. Sarratt had arrived from the Far East only an hour ago. He had slept on the plane, shaved, put on a clean shirt, looked fresh as a daisy. The Minister stared at him with active dislike.

'So fore-warned is not fore-armed?' he said.

'We—and the General—took a calculated risk.'

'And the responsibility.'

'The C.I.A. did,' Sarratt corrected. 'It was their show. You, sir, are our concern. We'll take better care of you.'

The Minister drummed his fingers on the desk. His doctor had given him pep pills that morning, after a sleepless night. The effect was beginning to wear off. Suddenly, he got up, unlocked a cupboard and took out a bottle of Scotch. He waved it at Sarratt who deemed it diplomatic to accept. The Minister gave Sarratt two fingers, himself four.

165

'You believe the killer's story—about working for the Russians?'

'No,' Sarratt said, 'I believe the original interpretation of the killings is right. The responsibility lies with an ultra left-wing, war-at-any-cost group in Peking. The missiles drop. The Chinese Commies—inheritors of the true creed—inherit the earth.'

'You could be mistaken. The tape could have been faked. Where's your proof?'

'The autopsy on the pianist,' Sarratt said. 'At the time of the concert he was high on heroin. He had cancer of the bowel and had less than six months to live.'

'So?'

'So it's easy to be a *kamikaze* when you're dying anyway. And something else, the piano player's wife's last known address, according to the best information available to the C.I.A., is Peking.'

'Too bad they didn't discover that before the killing.'

'As you say, sir.'

The Minister helped himself to another drink. This time he didn't offer Sarratt one, whose glass, anyway, was almost untouched. The Minister said, 'So many intangibles, so many possibilities for misinterpretation, for error.' With the alcohol, his tired brain was beginning to clear.

That made it easier for Sarratt. He waited until the Minister had paced the ministerial carpet, taken several more sips of ministerial Scotch. Then he said, 'Now, sir, we must discuss your own personal situation.'

The other nodded.

'You realize the date mentioned for your assassination is exactly one week from today?'

'Of course.' The voice was now standard English, not the manufactured-in-Birmingham accent, carefully calculated to impress constituents and the nation. 'What's your recommendation?'

'You put yourself unreservedly in our hands.'

166

'Meaning?'

'We treat your body, your person, exactly as if it were a thing. Something that can be put in a safe deposit vault, locked away, preserved like a mummy, a work of art.'

The Minister looked at him, trying to detect the contempt, the mockery. He saw nothing but a bland, expressionless, well-shaven countenance.

'You realize these are days of the utmost crisis, that my presence is needed here in Whitehall, in Westminster? I'm a Minister of the Crown?'

Sarratt said quietly, 'There's a time in every man's life when health must take precedence over duty.'

The Minister stubbed out the old and lit a new cigarette. He inhaled deeply. At this moment he hated Sarratt more than ever. Not because of the harsh things he said, but because Sarratt, apparently deferential, subservient, was in fact, the boss.

Sarratt was the ultimate power. And what the Minister had wanted, all his life, since bullying other kids at school, and getting firsts at university, and jockeying for position among hundreds, thousands, as he fought his way up through the labyrinthine corridors of the party, was power.

Not the trappings, the pomp, the pageantry. Not the title—pleasant though it might be. But the knowledge that: 'When I ope my mouth, let no dog bark!'

Sarratt kept silent. He could follow, as if by telepathy, every nuance of the other's thought, calculation. To withdraw from the political arena now when ultimate power, the premiership itself, was within his grasp, was tantamount to political suicide. There was no convenient record of ill-health on which to draw. If he suddenly vanished from the scene now, to be put in security cold-storage, the jackals would rejoice. He would be a dead duck. His chances of the highest office gone for ever.

167

A life-time of diligent chiselling thrown away, the endless committee sessions pointless. Exhaustion battled with ambition and impotent rage.

'Why,' he demanded out loud, 'why did they have to pick on me?'

Sarratt, personally, could think of a no more expendable politician. But he said, 'Just the bad luck of the draw, sir. Your name came up.'

The Minister stopped pacing, sat behind the immense desk, entrenched, his confidence and optimism returning as the liquor did its work.

'May I take it you'll put yourself unreservedly in our charge?'

'Damn it! Confounded impertinence! You may not!' the Minister shouted in a voice worthy of a larger audience. 'I shall carry out my public duties in whatever way circumstances demand. You, and the other security forces of the Crown, will provide the maximum protection possible having regard to these circumstances.'

He spoke as if dictating a memorandum.

Sarratt nodded. 'Very well, sir. If that's your wish.'

'It is.'

'Maximum security precautions will be applied immediately.'

A shadow passed over the Minister's face. For days, ever since the crisis blew up, he had not seen, or even phoned, Kathy, the girl friend who had once been his secretary and who was now comfortably installed in a high-rent Kensington flat. For days the Minister had been thinking of Kathy's voluptuous charms, for days (and nights) he had lain awake worrying about how she was spending her time—and with whom. Kathy bored easily.

'You said a week,' the Minister said. 'The killers, so far, have always operated exactly on schedule. Why should they change the *modus operandi* just for me?'

Sarratt shrugged. He saw the other's point. More accurately, looking at the Minister in his rather crumpled grey suit, he suddenly saw him in pyjamas *couleur de rose*.

He said blandly, 'Well, sir, shall we say maximum security starts in three days?' He said it like a headmaster announcing a holiday.

'Three days.' The Minister nodded, picked up some official document from his desk, and gave it minute attention though his eyes did not focus on a single word. 'Thank you, Sarratt.'

Sarratt withdrew. Outside in the lobby, he instructed one of his men to keep the Minister under surveillance, as usual. Discreet, unobtrusive.

On the other side of the door, the Minister tossed the document aside. Suddenly, uncontrollably, tears of self-pity and fatigue welled from his eyes.

Chapter Seventeen

Steiner introduced her as a 'very perceptive, very well-connected, very charming young newspaper correspondent from our great protector, the United States'. This in his best avuncular, fund-raising style.

Anna put a big trusting smile on her face and said, 'Hi!'

There were twenty of them, including four wives. Sixteen key men. Over the last few hours they had flown into Frankfurt from Britain, France, Spain, the United States, South America, North Africa, Malaysia, Australia and half a dozen other countries, as well as Western Germany itself.

For international delegates, they presented a singularly uniform appearance. These people did not come originally from the four corners of the globe, but from a relatively small area of Central and Eastern Europe. She caught snatches of Czech, German, Rumanian, Croat, Hungarian. They looked mid-European, acted mid-European.

Men, ostensibly of good will, of peace, yet because of fear, greed, ambition, lust for power, ready to wage war on humanity. Possibly the most dangerous collection of spies ever assembled under one roof.

Steiner's roof.

This was the pre-Congress get-together, all back-slapping and bonhomie, yet subdued, perhaps. Because of her?

Anna mixed, received untrusting smiles, polite, questioning raised eyebrows. They spoke in English, of varying degrees of proficiency, for her benefit—and in that language said nothing of significance.

Anna circulated, keeping her ears open. There was much speculation about where the Congress was to be held. Apparently, the venue every year was kept secret. The delegates assembled, the chartered plane took off. Excitement! The four wives had entirely new wardrobes for the occasion, and, uttering cries of pleasure, hated one another on sight.

A certain Madame Gora, apparently, was conspicuous by absence. A woman of charm, culture, refinement. But, alas, dead. Anna remembered the circumstances, the report of alcoholic-barbiturate suicide in a London paper. Gora the art dealer, greying, grave, immaculately tailored, received the commiserations of his fellow delegates.

Anna listened, smiled, asked the fatuous questions of a naïve reporter.

A fat man, a West German named Hugo, also circulated, drank, ate many canapes, smiled, joked with everyone. To Anna, he paid no attention at all.

Shadow fenced with shadow.

As the guests departed to their various hotels, Steiner approached Anna. He said, 'Anna, haven't you heard from Gino?'

'Is that likely? After the brush-off?'

'His flat's empty, he doesn't answer the phone at any of his usual haunts, his car's been found abandoned, by the police.'

Anna smiled mischievously the all-American-girl-smile. 'Maybe he's gone to find a more sympathetic public. Sunny Italy?'

'Maybe,' Steiner said. His answering smile was suspicious, unfriendly.

The chartered plane that took off from the Frankfurt field was a Dakota C47. Time 01.00 hours. The solitary stewardess spoke, haltingly, a number of languages with a German accent. She served Turkish coffee, thick, muddy and sweet, as the plane lumbered on its antiquated piston engines above the city, neon-glowing with the high blood-pressure flush of threatened prosperity.

The crisis news this evening was worse. The passengers settled back, somnolent after Steiner's lavish late supper at the airport restaurant.

Where this time? Tunis? Israel? Some Mediterranean island in the sun? Secrecy was the essential titillating condiment.

Anna dozed. The delegate beside her muttered incoherently in his sleep, a word or two of Croat which added up to nothing, except in the fantasies of the dreamer.

The landing, bumpy, short, dangerous, came in the half-light of dawn. Anna saw no navigation lights, no control tower, no airport buildings.

Sheer mountain walls reared up ahead, on either side. The plane came down like a lift.

The pilot knew his stuff.

Only one passenger knew where the plane was landing. Steiner. He knew because he had been there before, not because he had been briefed. Sudden fear touched his stomach like an icy hand. A surgeon called memory, probing for signs of death. Even the thought of Precious Emerald failed to warm him.

He glanced at his fellow-travellers, saw signs of unease, fear. All of them were seasoned travellers, knew what an airport, operating according to international regulations, looked like.

The stewardess was crouched in the tail, the safest place in a crash. No one had told them to fasten their safety-belts. If one broke one's teeth, displaced one's toupee, suffered from the sudden realization that man was not born to fly, here was one airline that simply did not care!

The plane bumped and rocked to a halt. The stewardess appeared from the tail, helped the delegates to the ground.

They looked around excitedly, pleased to be on solid earth, hugging their briefcases and their plastic macs. They found their voices, and by talking restored their self-esteem after the ego-deflating drama of the landing.

Steiner, like an experienced courier, took charge. Aided by the stewardess, he shepherded his flock towards the long, low, white building five hundred yards away.

Now there was no hanged man on the terrace, but in Steiner's brain one sensation was uppermost. Distaste, revulsion, dread. Three words for one gut-twisting feeling.

Anna slept. The depth of sleep varied. Now very deep, down in the unfathomable but serene Cousteau-world of green, evanescent marine wonders. Then to a place of turmoil, sickness and jagged, flesh-tearing rocks. The two worlds mingled.

Gasping for breath, half-drowned, she struggled ashore, clung to a slippery, seaweed-covered piece of stone and looked up, shaking the sea-water from her hair.

The Chinese girl looked down from the rock and smiled at her, holding a cup of coffee.

'Good sleep?'

Anna smiled back because the girl was cute, doll-like, irresistible, and tried to remember how it happened she was in this particular bed, in this particular place.

Particular place? What place? What country? To ask the routine, where-am-I question was unbearably corny. She looked round, sipping the excellent coffee. The room could be standard motel anywhere, comfortable, impersonal, good for any country, any climate.

Then she remembered the walk from the aircraft to the long, low white building, the delegates being received exactly as if checking in at a motel, and dispersing to their rooms.

Anna glanced at her wristwatch. Twelve o'clock. The Chinese girl drew the curtains and brilliant sunshine flooded the room. Twelve noon.

The plane had landed at about four a.m. Eight hours sleep like any honest, hard-working housewife.

The girl said, 'My name is Mia Hahn, which in English means Precious Emerald. I am at your command for the length of your stay.' She smiled and continued. 'There is no need for you to hurry. The delegates are just about to meet in private session. The meeting is expected to last about two hours. Then a communiqué will be issued to the press—another smile—'that is, to you. Mr Steiner sends his compliments and hopes you will join him later for drinks.' For a moment Anna almost imagined she was having a bed-borne privileged person's tour of the United Nations in New York.

'You are ready for your bath?'

'Thank you.'

'A pleasure.'

Precious Emerald made an obeisance and withdrew.

Anna got out of bed.

She looked out of the picture window, saw the narrow green valley, the towering mountains and the blue, blue sky. Five hundred yards away was the aircraft, like a fly somnolent in the sun. No people, nothing to indicate where she was. A view of extraordinary peace, yet here, if the signs were correct, 'the future' of the world was being planned after atomic war.

Precious Emerald came from the bathroom and bowed.

Anna said, 'I'm looking forward to meeting our host.'

Precious Emerald smiled, then hid her merriment quickly and discreetly behind her hand. 'Speak to host, yes. See him, no.'

'That's an odd kind of hospitality.'

'The wise man does not look upon the sun at midday.'

Anna was in no mood for Confucius in a cheongsan and went into the bathroom. Her arms and shoulders still hurt abominably.

The water was hot and fragrant, the soap sandalwood. She was, of course, quite unaware that, though denied sight of her host, he, at that moment, thanks to the impertinence of closed-circuit television, had an excellent view of her.

Seated behind his screen with Steiner in private audience the god said, 'The girl has no birth-mark on her left shoulder. There are deep red weals around her wrists, and she shows signs of pain, as if she has been subjected, very recently, to ill-use. Your operator must have been clumsy, stupid.'

'The Italian is exceptionally clever where women are concerned.'

'Then this woman must be even cleverer, and also possessed of great courage.' The god paused. 'You did right to bring her here. Spy or naïve American, we must see what use can be made of her. Here, at least, she can do no harm during these critical days.'

'Any fresh developments?' Steiner asked.

'The situation has worsened—or improved,' the god said, 'according to one's point of view. The Americans have demanded the arrest and public trial of those responsible for the assassination of their General, which, of course, the Russians cannot do, even if they thought it politically desirable, because, as we both know *they* didn't kill him. There is talk of an ultimatum. There could be war within three days.' The god sounded pleased.

Steiner felt sick. His game was cold war, not hot, infinitely and profitably prolonged. Spies have a vested interest in uneasy peace. Also, last night, or rather, at

175

dawn, he had been reunited with Mrs S., an unnerving, depressing experience.

Apparently she had spent most of the last two weeks painting her nails, toe and finger, and dallying with an Arab boy of astonishing versatility, thoughtfully provided by what she called 'the management', for whom she now had great appreciation, though she had only spoken to, never seen, the god.

'War possibly within three days,' the god was saying, 'especially if the third assassination goes according to plan. The British Minister, by the way, is making a fine show of devotion to duty. In Parliament he has declared himself ready to fly anywhere in the world, meet anyone in the cause of peace and understanding. The clichés politicians use.'

Steiner said, 'That could be awkward if his assassination is to take place on schedule.'

'I think not. I have arranged for him to have a travelling companion.' The god's voice hardened. 'The assassination must and will take place. The first killing could have been merely lucky, the second inspired improvisation. The third must demonstrate our infallibility. The Minister must die.'

General war? Steiner tried to visualize the prospect. No America, no Russia, no Europe. He liked travelling about, expense accounts, the good life, power. Frankly, he didn't see much of a future for himself in China.

'Just how will the British Minister be eliminated?' Steiner asked.

'That is my secret,' the god said, 'a little exercise in long-range control.'

Steiner shrugged. If this one was exclusively the god's pigeon, so much the better. No responsibility if things went wrong.

After a moment's silence, the god said, 'Let us now turn our attention to the present business. The delegates will assemble here in this room. The meeting will be conducted by you. I, of course, will remain silent, invisible. You will guide the meeting to bring out the character of each man, so that I may assess his potentialities. You will impress upon the delegates that they are an élite. Appeal to their vanity, their cupidity. For his own sake, I hope each man will make a correct impression. Otherwise, elimination will be ruthless.'

The god fell silent behind the grille. Steiner waited.

After a few moments the door opened and the delegates entered, ushered in, Steiner saw with quickening interest, by Precious Emerald. The girl stood at the threshold, head bowed deferentially, giving no sign of recognition.

The delegates seemed relaxed, pleased with their surroundings. Yet each man sensed this was an extraordinary occasion. A time of trial.

The room now had a large oval table and Western-style chairs. There was a card bearing each man's name at each chair, a scribbling pad, ball-points, a carafe containing, presumably, water. The water, however, did contain a large measure of 120-proof vodka, tasteless, odourless, known to be particularly effective in loosening men's tongues.

Steiner looked round at the assembled faces. Gora from London, Hegedus from New York, Brusa from Ankara, Brasnov from Rome, Mallik from Stockholm. He glanced at the delegates from Buenos Aires, from Cape Town, Addis Ababa, the last a particularly wily Rumanian who had already supplied valuable information about uranium deposits in Ethiopia and the pro-Chinese sympathies of certain politicians in Egypt and the Sudan.

There were men from Ottawa, Mexico City, Teheran, Helsinki. From Singapore, Melbourne, Tokyo and Belgrade. The man from Melbourne, a one-time East German rocket expert who had 'escaped' to the West in 1947 and was engaged on missile experiments in the Australian outback, had been within the last twelve months, a particularly valuable recruit.

They were mostly men in their forties and fifties, well-tailored, showing an immaculate inch of cuff, smelling of pre-shave, after-shave and various other lotions designed to mask, conceal, or even deny the physical nature of man.

They were fundamentally as alike as a bunch of ad-men from Manhattan, fox-hunting men from the English shires, or intellectuals from the Left Bank.

Steiner remained seated and tapped with his signet ring on a glass. The subdued hum of conversation in half a dozen languages ceased. Steiner spoke in English.

'Gentlemen, our host, who wishes as usual to remain anonymous, bids you welcome, and trusts you have relaxed after your journey and find your accommodation agreeable.' There was a murmur of assent. 'The precise location of our meeting this year must remain secret, and I apologize for the atmosphere of mystery that surrounds this place. No doubt many of you will be able to make inspired guesses about where you are at this moment—I should be disappointed in your abilities if you were not!—but a mystery it must remain. This year there will be none of the customary entertainments and excursions usually laid on by our host country. Gentlemen, there is no time for them. It is a time of crisis. The international situation is on the boil. At any moment there may be war. This Organization will become more important than ever before.

'Important to whom? That question is, no doubt, in your minds. As agents of the Organization, you are my employees, answerable only to me. To whom I am responsible you do not know! Let me tell you only this. If war does indeed break out—involving Russia and the West—a war neither side can possibly win—then you, gentlemen, will not be on the losing side.

'Gentlemen, you will notice that I have said nothing about our activities as a front Organization as it is known to thousands of sentimentalists and intellectuals all over the

178

world. The prestige we enjoy among such people and governments attests to your success in preserving and fostering the
correct image of the Organization. No time will be wasted,
therefore, on that important but entirely secondary—
though often pleasant and remunerative—aspect of our
work. This meeting will be concerned only with your real
achievements in espionage during the last few months at
each centre, with immediate prospects, work in progress. I
shall call on each centre head to make his report in turn,
starting with Francis Gora, head of our Organization in
London.'

Steiner took a sip of water, looked directly at Gora. 'But
first let me express the sentiments, I am sure, of everyone
present in assuring our colleague of our deep and sincere
sympathy in his recent tragic loss. Certain members' wives
have, I know, been of immense value to us. Mrs Gora will be
greatly missed. Gentlemen, never underestimate the power
of a woman. Take good care of your wives!'

The delegates murmured their assent and agreement,
and took the hint.

Gora rose, expressed his thanks, then launched immediately into an account of the British centre's activities during
the year. His voice shook a little, not with grief, but with
apprehension. No such meeting at which the real objectives
of the Organization were so openly discussed, had ever
previously been called. His every instinct told him this was a
test, a trial.

'I will begin,' he said, 'with my discovery of the precise
locations of three of Great Britain's emergency food stores
for use in the event of a nuclear attack. . . .'

Why? The question kept nagging at him as he was speaking, upsetting his chain of thought, the cogency of his ex-
position. Why break security like this, even among the most
important of his colleagues in the Organization.

Information of the kind he was now giving should be
passed from private mouth to private ear, in a whisper.

179

Why break this rule? Why now? Why? His words faltered. Sweat trickled down his sides from his armpits.

Steiner was staring at him fixedly. 'You are feeling ill, Gora? You are finding the mental and physical strain of possessing this knowledge too great?'

Gora shook his head. 'I am perfectly well. Perfectly.' He took a sip of water. 'The caves in the Pennine hills,' he said, 'are to be used principally for the storage of sugar and tea. Apparently the British cannot envisage life even in the post-nuclear world without that beverage!'

He glanced around at his fellow delegates, hoping for a smile, but was not rewarded. His tension had communicated itself to them.

'No comment, if you please!' Steiner said. 'Confine yourself to facts.'

'I apologize!' Gora mopped his forehead. 'The tea is entirely Indian. The great mass of the British people do not like the Chinese variety. . . .'

Chapter Eighteen

Anna lay in the scented water and considered the position. Her assignment was to worm herself as close to Steiner as possible. This, in a measure, she had done. Afterwards? It was up to her. Her initiative alone.

Here she was under the same roof as the world's most formidable collection of spies, evidently gathered for a kind of espionage congress. One girl against the lot. And the roof was obviously somewhere in the depths of the Balkans, probably Albania, if the Chinese girl was anything to go by.

A wild scheme began to form itself in her head. She had flown in with the party, and would, presumably, if Steiner didn't eliminate her, fly out with it.

So? She had taken flying lessons in a Piper Cub, but piloting a C47 with a hostile crew and passengers breathing down her neck was likely to be a brief and disastrous exploit. However, if she could make the crew fly the plane in the direction she ordered—without the passengers being aware. . . .

Anna soaped her stomach and thought of the weapons at her disposal.

There was her own gun—a small but deadly model, standard issue, according to Sarratt, to British lady spies. The weapon easily dismantled and was in fact carried in that state in her beauty-box. The barrel looked like a fancy lipstick container and she used it every day to make-up. The butt and magazine also doubled as a powder compact. The bullets were in a perfectly good tin of talcum powder fitted with a false bottom.

The gun was a useful gadget, able to escape any but the most thorough and expert examination of her belongings. But would it inspire respect in the hostile crew of the plane? Would they simply laugh at her? Would she be forced to shoot one of them to prove her point? When it came to the point, would she be able to?

She also had a nailfile like a stiletto—useless for such a plan.

Perhaps it had been a mistake to throw Gino's gun after him into the pit. That weapon at least carried conviction.

Anna got out of the bath, wrapped herself in a huge Turkish towel and went into the bedroom.

The Chinese girl was standing beside the window, the beauty-box open beside her, the compact-cum-magazine in her hand. She was examining it closely, seemed unaware Anna had entered.

Anna hesitated only a fraction of a second, then as the girl looked up, smiled. 'You like it?'

'Oh, yes. Yes. Very much.' From the girl's expression it was impossible to say whether her appreciation was for a neat little gimmick of espionage or a harmless feminine trifle.

'Try the powder,' Anna said. She took the barrel out of the beauty-box. 'And the lipstick.'

The girl's eyes sparkled. She really was a cute thing. As devious and dangerous as herself?

Anna watched carefully, smiling, as she manipulated the compact and the lipstick with apparently unaccustomed fingers. She noticed the girl wore no make-up herself, only a heavy perfume. Her skin was flawless, like golden ivory.

Anna said, 'It must be difficult for a Chinese girl living here to get things like that from the West. I'd make you a present of them, but those are things a girl just can't do without when she's travelling.'

Precious Emerald held the compact in one hand, now the lipstick in the other. Was she wondering how the two fitted together? Then she smiled prettily. 'Of course. I understand.'

What did she understand? Anna went to her suitcase, quickly rummaged through her belongings, found a new nylon nightie, very chic, very provocative, from Sachs, Fifth Avenue, and offered it to the girl. 'For you.'

Briefly, Precious Emerald's fingers caressed the material. Then she drew back, shaking her head as if suddenly afraid to speak. Their eyes met—was Anna mistaken in thinking in the girl's there was a hint of uncertainty, perhaps even a warning?

Precious Emerald bowed, murmured, 'I will attend later,' and was gone.

What had happened in the last twenty seconds to change the girl's manner? Had she detected something suspicious about Anna or her possessions? Or was the room bugged, and had her ears detected some minute electronic indication of it which Anna's had missed? More dangerous still, were they also being watched?

Anna let the towel fall from her and began to dress. As she did so her eyes wandered round the room. There were at least half a dozen places where a miniature microphone could be concealed, two or three that would accommodate a wide-angle lens.

If she were giving a performance, Anna decided to make it a good one. *The Foggy, Foggy Dew*, sung with charming huskiness.

The first session was over, and the god was amusing himself by switching from room to room, examining his guests.

But he kept coming back to this girl. He found her fascinating. A better body than that of his cast-off Italian mistress he had used to intimidate Steiner in Corfu. Much more versatile, he guessed, than Precious Emerald, of whom he was beginning to tire anyway and using more and more to test and entertain his guests—a sure sign of impending boredom as far as his relations with women were concerned.

This one he would take pleasure in bending to his will. All the women he had used till now, both personally and professionally, had been either Oriental or from European nations with a long history of female subservience to male. With such women there was little satisfaction in conquest. It was too easy. Resistance was as important in the bedroom as a texture in food at the table that gave resistance to the teeth.

For a moment, the god allowed his attention to be distracted nostalgically by the thought of the flesh of a certain snake, prepared only by his own cook in Peking. The cook foisted upon him at this outlandish station was a barbarian, and he anticipated his meals with little pleasure. Still, with this new girl to amuse him. . . . The god's face softened a little. Of course he would keep that fool Steiner guessing about what he intended to do with her, but watching her now as she pulled first one stocking then the other up each shapely leg, his mind was made up.

Suddenly, on the console, a small yellow light flashed repeatedly. The god frowned, but at once turned off the sight and sound of Anna. He picked up a green telephone, gave the code sentence of recognition of the day in Chinese, and listened.

Now and then he asked a question. His expression became set, hard. Though his voice was calm, obedient, even deferential, the corners of his mouth drooped in soured contempt. What he had feared, anticipated, provided for, had come to pass.

When he hung up, for a long moment he sat frozen in contemplation, like a Buddha indeed.

At last he rose and passed into his own simple personal apartment which was separated from the monitor and communications room by an armoured door like that of a safe, and of which only he had the combination.

He scarcely seemed aware of Precious Emerald's presence as she stood deferentially bowing to receive him. To the god she was part of the furniture, such is the capacity of man to become indifferent to the beauty of a particular woman.

'Well?'

'I found nothing about the girl to indicate she is not what she appears to be, an American journalist.'

The god sucked his teeth. Precious Emerald was a fool and a liar, a constant reminder of the inefficiency of the school devoted to the training of female agents in Peking. The graduates might, perhaps, have their uses in dealing with fellow Orientals, in South East Asia, for instance. But against Europeans and Americans, about whom they had only book knowledge, hopeless—as transparently, obviously ingenuous as an Intourist guide in Russia.

The god permitted himself to glance at Precious Emerald as a woman for the last time. His eye passed over every inch of the body that had once given him so much pleasure. Now he felt only distaste.

'So you have nothing to report?'

'Only that she tried to give me a Western woman's undergarment. As a present, a gesture of good will, not a bribe.'

'You took it?'

The god knew of course the answer, but *pro forma* the question had to be asked.

Precious Emerald shook her head. 'To receive such a gift would be uncultured, unworthy of a daughter of the Chinese People's revolution.'

The god nodded, bored rather than approving. 'It is we who make gifts to the Westerners. Tonight you will make a gift of yourself to such of our guests as I shall indicate later. Their minds must be kept from thought. You understand?'

'I understand.'

Precious Emerald bowed and withdrew.

The god assumed the lotus-position. Yoga he used not as a religious exercise, merely as an effective way of bringing mind and body under perfect control, enabling him to make decisions uncoloured by irritation, anger, nervous strain or bodily fatigue. As he performed the breathing exercises, his face became completely calm, mask-like.

Half an hour later he had worked out to the last detail what to do. The subtlety of his decisions amused him, brought him inner content, like an intricate mathematical problem solved. His countenance was now benign. He manipulated the combination lock on the steel door and returned to the control and communications chamber.

He pressed a switch. The Steiners were arguing about money again. She was worrying about whether he had been wasting it during her enforced vacation. Mrs S. regarded the whole business as a way of preparing for a prosperous old age. The god smiled sardonically.

Brought up on Muzac, public address systems in every hotel, airport and supermarket she had ever frequented, Mrs S. had adapted to his method of disembodied communication well. The god sensed she had even come to like him. With reason. He had anticipated her every wish. He would give her a very special parting gift—not to be opened till the plane left.

The god pressed another button which rang Steiner's phone. Mrs S. answered it. 'Why hello, there! Thanks again for the marvellous lunch!'

The god said, feeling ridiculous, like a head-waiter, 'I'm glad you enjoyed it, Mrs Steiner. May I speak with your husband?'

'Why, sure.'

Edwin came out of the bathroom in striped cotton underpants.

'There has been a change of plan,' the god said. 'The meeting must end tonight.'

'Tonight?' Steiner was astonished. 'Why? What's happened? The balloon's gone up?'

'Meaning war? No, not that. Not yet. But you will obey orders, Mr Steiner, without comment, as I obey mine. You will say nothing to the meeting of this change of plan, but simply do everything necessary, as chairman, to see that all relevant business is transacted at the latest by ten p.m. There will be one short break at seven p.m. for further refreshment. When the meeting is wound up, the members will disperse to their rooms. At midnight the plane will take off.'

'What destination?' Steiner sounded worried.

'Frankfurt, naturally. The meeting will resume in ten minutes. As before, of course, I shall be watching, listening.'

'The girl?' Steiner said. 'What about the girl?'

'She will be dealt with by me, personally,' the god told him.

Chapter Nineteen

The pilot stood rigidly to attention before the grille and the invisible god. An ex-flyer of the Foreign Legion and once an ace in the Luftwaffe, he was paid by the Chinese twice as much as a senior pilot of Pan-Am.

For this he was expected to obey every directive without question, take any risk.

'Repeat your orders,' the god said.

'At eleven fifty-nine a.m. I take off from here, fly to a military airfield in Egypt, south-east of Cairo, where the plane will be refuelled. I get air-borne again as soon as practicable, fly down the Red Sea, then cross Saudi Arabia, avoiding the British airfield at Bahrein. I then fly at low level across Iran to a secret airstrip in Afghanistan, west of Kabul.'

'Correct! Naturally, the airstrip is maintained without Russian or American knowledge.'

'After refuelling, I continue to one of the many Chinese-maintained airstrips in Tibet, then fly across metropolitan China to Peking, as ordered. At each and every stop, no passenger will be permitted to leave the aircraft. During flight the passengers will be guarded by six armed men with orders to kill if any passenger becomes insubordinate or in any way endangers the safety of the aircraft.'

'Correct! You yourself, Captain, will select these six men from the garrison here, brief them thoroughly, and be personally responsible for them. Arrangements are already being made by Peking to ensure the aircraft is strongly guarded by local troops wherever it lands for fuel. But there must be no incidents that might embarrass our friends. Only when the plane finally lands at a military airfield near Peking will your responsibility end. Any incident which causes the Chinese Government to lose face will mean your instant execution, without trial.'

'I understand, Excellency.'

'It will be a long flight, Captain. You have complete confidence in your co-pilot and radio-officer? While you sleep, they will do their duty?'

'Have no fear on that score, Excellency.'

'It is for you to fear, Captain. Any failing of theirs will be considered your own.'

The pilot drew himself up even more stiffly.

'You will see to it that enough food, water and such luxuries as wines, liqueurs, cigarettes and cigars are taken aboard the aircraft and served during flight. The girl Precious Emerald will wait upon the passengers. One or two of the soldiers will dress as stewards in appropriate white jackets. The rest will wear civilian clothes, passing as businessmen or diplomats. Select men who will be convincing in these roles. Use discretion.This is a precious human cargo. For as long as possible treat them as honoured guests. Inevitably, as time passes and they reach no European destination, they will become restive. But handle them with kindness rather than force. The girl Precious Emerald will help in this. She has long been conditioned to complete obedience. Have you any questions?'

'Only one, Excellency. What action am I to take if intercepted by Allied or Russian fighter aircraft and ordered to land?'

'The aircraft is fitted with very long-range fuel tanks, is it not?'

'Yes, Excellency.'

'Then you will avoid all areas where Russian fighters are known to patrol. If you are intercepted by Allied fighters, you will identify yourself as a chartered transport plane carrying a party of tourists. On no account must you land. The British and Americans do not make a habit of firing upon transport aircraft. But as far as possible, you will fly far away from the main areas of patrol, Russian, British or American. You are familiar with these areas. In this, as in all other matters concerning the flight, you will use the utmost discretion.' The god fell silent. Then, 'You have much to do, Captain, before midnight. Set about it.'

'Excellency!'

The Captain saluted his invisible commander behind the grille and withdrew.

A small smile played around the features of the god. His instructions to the pilot had been meticulous, detailed. He had carried out Peking's orders to the letter.

If anything should go wrong, who, in the smallest degree, could hold him responsible?

It was a little after two p.m. In fifteen minutes Steiner would resume the meeting.

In the communications control-room, the god spent the time tuning quickly to half a dozen newscasts all round the world: New York, Paris, London, Moscow, Rome, Buenos Aires. According to national temperament, the speakers were calm, excited, hysterical.

But the facts were the same. The news was out.

A peace conference was to start in three days. In Tirana, capital of 'neutral' Albania—the Chinese attending as observers.

One of these observers—though the newscasters did not mention this—would be the god himself!

What loss of face! What humiliation! From master-spy,

a real manipulator of events, controller of destinies, human and political, to a mere observer! To see his Organization, built up over years, become the plaything of the bureaucrats of Peking!

This, at least, he could prevent.

But to witness the triumph of the moderates in Peking was depressing. Infinitely so. Chinese Communism was going the same way as the Russian variety. The meek would inherit the earth.

Here, at least for the moment, he was still supreme. Here, in this valley.

At random, pressing key after key, he glanced at several delegates awaiting in their rooms the call to the next session.

They were resting, reading, chatting with their wives. Except Havas, the Latin-American delegate, a Spanish physicist who had made the useful discovery that a certain South American state was trying to build a bomb—because he happened to be working on it! Havas wasn't a very good nuclear scientist, but he was the best that particular state could afford. Also, he was *persona grata* in top political circles, had built up a useful espionage network among *émigré* Europeans in the South American continent, and knew what was going on.

The god frowned. Havas was listening to a news broadcast from Rome on a small transitor radio. If he spoke of the Tirana conference to any of the other delegates, they would become inhibited, puzzled, even rebellious. It was essential for them to think the world on the brink of war, not of peace.

The god pressed another switch.

The Chinese commander of the garrison answered at once. The god said, 'My orders were that the luggage and persons of each of our guests were to be searched for miniature radios. Yet at this moment the guest in Room 17 is listening to one. He will be seized immediately, and the man responsible for carrying out the search, hanged, at once and in private.'

'Yes, Excellency!'

The god continued to watch Havas in Room 17. The Spaniard was listening to the Rome broadcast with mounting excitement, excitedly pacing the room.

According to Reuter and Associated Press, a prominent member of the British Delegation to the Tirana Conference would be the Cabinet Minister, William Hobbs: he would be accompanied by Mrs Hobbs. The names of the Russian and American delegates had not yet been announced. Tirana, the newscast continued, was wild with excitement. The conference would end the country's long period of isolation. Though the capital lacked many amenities associated with international conference centres, immense efforts were being made to provide comfortable accommodation. The meetings themselves would be held in a summer palace once owned by King Zog. . . .

Havas turned suddenly as the door opened. Two soldiers seized his arms, a third covered his mouth with a gag and at the same time jabbed a hypodermic needle into his arm.

For a few seconds Havas struggled violently, then went limp. He was laid upon a folding stretcher, carried from the room.

Fortunately, Havas had completed his report that morning. His presence at the meeting was no longer necessary.

The god pressed yet another switch and spoke to Steiner. 'The Spaniard Havas has, unfortunately, become ill,' he said. 'Probably some gastric trouble. Stomach pains, fever, most distressing. This afternoon's session will start at once without him.'

'Poor guy!' Steiner said. He knew better than to ask questions.

In the control-room, the god put a new spool of tape into the recorder ready for the new session. The reports already made had been highly satisfactory, covering England, North and South America and France. The value of the tape on which they were recorded was incalculable.

The god started the machine. Over the loudspeaker, with pin-sharp clarity, came the voice of Steiner calling the meeting to order.

Pale starlight bathed the valley and the surrounding peaks. From her window, Anna could make out the plane. A jeep stood beside it. Men passed boxes from the vehicle into the belly of the plane.

The aircraft's tanks were also being laboriously filled from drums with a hand-pump. A mechanic had been working on the motors during the afternoon. Clearly, something was on. Something more, she guessed, than a mere routine flight of a few hundred miles back to Frankfurt.

Earlier, she had been allowed to walk in the carefully tended garden, but when she had ventured farther a young man she suspected was Albanian, smiling but firm, had gestured her back. When she had spoken to him in English and sign language, indicating her wish to go farther afield, he had merely shrugged and smiled, and shepherded her back to the building.

Of her fellow-passengers from Frankfurt all day there had been no sign. Except for Steiner. He had put in a brief appearance, told her there would be no communiqué for the time being, owing to pressure of work. 'Just relax. Take things easy. You'll get a story.'

Steiner didn't look relaxed himself. He had a strained, hunted look. When he patted her arm, his hand shook. She smelt liquor on his breath. Steiner, the do-gooder who only drank milk.

After the intense heat of the day, the night was surprisingly cold. Anna kicked off her shoes and lay on the bed fully dressed, nerves taut, listening. Beside her on the bed was her beauty-box, open, the lipstick container and the powder compact only inches away.

Mentally she rehearsed the precise movements necessary

to assemble and load the gun, movements she had practised many times back at the studio in Kent.

Best time, working entirely by touch in the dark, twenty seconds.

Then she practised relaxation, starting with her toes, muscle by muscle, legs, belly, chest, the expression on her face.

She was in fact smiling slightly when she became aware that the door was opening, not fully, just enough to admit someone.

Then the door closed again, soundlessly, and it seemed that no one had come in. Anna's hand snaked silently towards the beauty-box. If there was no chance to use the gun, the long nailfile made a useful weapon. Her fingers closed around it.

A moment later, Precious Emerald was beside her in the bed, pulling the sheet to cover them both. The Chinese girl took Anna in her arms and pressed her lips to her ear.

'Do not speak,' she whispered. 'Listen. I know you are a spy. Everyone here knows. Do not reach for that little gun you use to paint your lips and powder your face. Do not stab me with the nailfile. I wish you no harm. I am your friend. I wish to help you. I come to you like this, as a lover, because everything in this room may be watched, heard.'

Anna in her turn brushed her mouth against the other's ear. 'Why? Why should you help me?'

'Because you are alone. Because you are a woman. Because I am to die and I wish to be revenged. Listen carefully. Soon the plane will take off, with everyone aboard who came here, except you. I shall also be aboard, soldiers, too. The plane is going far away, perhaps as far as China. This I know because the mighty one who is my master thinks I am a foolish girl. He does not know that I have the knowledge to spy on him—and instructions from Peking to do so.'

A dozen questions occurred to Anna. But the Chinese girl

said, 'Be silent little one. Soon I must leave you. The plane will never reach Peking. This I am sure of because I know the mighty one. Never, never will he permit those who serve him to serve others. But everything that has been said by those you travelled with has been recorded. The mighty one has the tapes. If, somehow, you could escape from this valley with the tapes . . . Soon he will send for you. Though he knows you are an enemy spy, you please him. . . .'

Precious Emerald drew Anna even closer to herself. 'If you can escape, little one,' she whispered, 'go south across the mountains. There you will find friends.'

For a brief moment, the girl's lips touched Anna's cheeks. 'I have never known love from a man,' she said. 'Perhaps I could have loved you, little one.'

Then she was gone.

Soon he will send for you. Obviously, any idea of highjacking the plane with her toy-pistol was out. She wasn't going to be allowed to even board the plane.

Anna lay still, strangely excited, trembling. The scent of Precious Emerald still clung to the pillow. When, half an hour later, she rose, the door was locked.

Anna glanced at her watch. Two minutes to midnight. Unnaturally loud in the immense silence, came the sound of a motor starting up. She moved to the window.

Below, the delegates were being ushered into a car. Anna recognized Precious Emerald, neat, capable, chic, as she aided them like an air hostess.

Several times the car went from villa to aircraft. Mr and Mrs Steiner were in the last party. There was no sign of force. The occasion had every appearance of a routine trip.

Silence again. Then the engines of the plane came to life, reverberating with an ear-splitting din against the walls of the valley. To anyone but a stunt pilot the hazards of the take-off would have seemed impossible. But the pilot knew his stuff. The old Dakota seemed to lift off the non-existent runway as if hauled up on an invisible string, its rate of climb more like that of a jet than a piston-engined aircraft. Anna suspected very-special, non-standard engines.

The din died away quickly, and Anna felt more alone, deserted, desolated, than till this moment she had believed possible. She missed Steiner, especially she missed Precious Emerald. Friends? Enemies? No matter, just the possibility of human contact.

She decided one shot of Johnnie Walker in her present unbearable loneliness was not self-indulgent but medicinal. Just three fingers taken with ice and Perrier.

Anna savoured the liquor slowly, and felt the awful depression lift from her brain and spirit. She tried the door again and found it still locked. Was this the time to assemble the gun? Everything considered, she thought not. It was inconceivable she would be ushered into the presence of the so-called mighty one unsearched.

Again she lay on the bed, waited. The luminous hands of her Longines moved to half an hour after midnight.

Then, silently, the door opened, the lights were switched on. Two smiling Chinese, dressed in white jackets like waiters, stood on the threshold. Anna had never seen them before.

'You will come, please?'

Anna got off the bed, slipped her feet into her shoes.

She said, 'Come where?' But the Chinese only smiled. She smiled back.

They stood aside, waiting for her to precede them. Anna moved to the door, then, as if she had forgotten something, went back to the bed and picked up her beauty-box.

One of the Chinese beat her to it. He grabbed the box and tipped its contents on to the bed. He picked up each feminine trifle, examined it as if it contained the secret of eternal life, his face suddenly hard, impassive.

When he came to the lipstick, Anna took it from him, showed him how it worked on her mouth. Then she took a

196

small flacon of Tabac Blonde, unstoppered it, and dabbed a few drops on her arm and let him smell.

He drew back as if tasting forbidden fruit. The master's woman was evidently not for the common soldier. He grinned sheepishly, nodded, understood. The beauty-box was part of the feminine armoury, acceptable, necessary, pleasing to the mighty one.

When she stepped out of the room, the soldier carried it for her like a relic capable of miracles.

Down one corridor, then another. A locked door. One of the Chinese stayed behind here, and Anna went on, down another short corridor accompanied only by the bearer of the beauty-box.

Another locked door. The Chinese, now almost on hands and knees in humility, ushered Anna into the room beyond. The door closed almost at once, and she was alone, the beauty-box before her on a low table.

Anna looked around curiously. A monastic cell? Whitewashed walls, a simple bed, plain wooden desk and chair. Hardly the room of a sybarite. The lair of a meglomaniac, a mystic, a saint, a scholar? Possibly. Also, it reminded her of Holloway, the prison.

The most remarkable feature of the room was a steel door, high as a small man, like that of a safe. Behind it, what? The ultimate mystery? A tomb?

Anna waited. Minutes passed.

She decided this was the moment to assemble the gun. To steady her nerves, she timed the operation. Twenty-five seconds. She noticed her hands were steady and dry. Good!

Then she saw the steel door opening.

The man who came into the room was completely bald. He wore a single white cloth draped about his body like a fakir. Perched on his nose was a pair of steel-rimmed spectacles. His features were entirely smooth, like an infant's, except that down the left cheek, from temple to chin, was a deep and ancient scar, souvenir of some frightful wound.

His teeth seemed perfectly white, though when he smiled, as he did now, looking at her, there was a hint of gold.

The scar and the smile produced the effect of a gargoyle. Though undoubtedly Chinese, he said in a cultured English voice, 'I am seventy-five years old and you will be the seventy-fifth woman I have possessed. I hope you will be worthy of the occasion.'

Suddenly, uncontrollably, Anna began to laugh. She laughed until the tears came.

The smile vanished from the face of the god. He stood, quite motionless, watching her.

Anna's laughter ceased as suddenly as it had begun, like an unpredictable fit of hysteria. Her hand reached for the tiny gun. Then the god struck her with such force that she fell against the whitewashed wall. She felt a warm trickle of blood run from her nose. The violence of his assault had been completely unexpected.

He waited for her to get to her feet. She saw his arm raised to strike again. Instinctively, she transferred her weight to meet and counter the attack.

It did not come. Across the face of the god there passed a look of immense bewilderment as if some deeper insult had been offered to his divinity even than her laughter.

The features froze then, in a grimace of pain. He tottered forward, clutched at her and fell.

It took the god two minutes to die. Anna waited and watched. His eyes remained fixed upon her. No words came, no plea for help.

A heart attack, undoubtedly!

When she was quite sure he was dead, Anna took a pad and mascara from her beauty-box and carefully took fingerprints from each hand. With her miniature camera she took photographs of the face, full and profile.

The dead eyes of the god watched her every movement, saw her open the steel door which was still ajar.

Anna photographed the equipment, then quickly looked

through the collection of tapes, all numbered. She played back a few feet of the spool on the recorder. A voice, in middle-European English, said . . . 'This new rocket fuel developed by the Americans advances their space programme by two years.'

Then Steiner's voice said, 'The names of your contacts in Washington and New Mexico?'

The first voice mentioned three names.

Anna switched off the machine, put the tape and the three numbered preceding spools into her beauty-box—as many as it would carry.

Then she saw a device on the wall of the chamber like a clock. It seemed to have no relevance to any of the recording, radio or other electronic equipment. From it two wires led to a metal plate in the floor, secured by two screws.

Anna found a small screwdriver and removed the plate. She had learned enough about explosives at the studio to recognize a bomb, some destruction gimmick.

She replaced the plate, then set the clock going to a ten-minute deadline, pressed a small red switch.

The god was still watching as she came back into the cell. Anna firmly gripped the beauty-box in her left hand, the toy pistol in her right. She tapped on the door with her shoe, then stood back.

The door opened, and one of the Chinese entered. He uttered a cry and stared stupidly at the dead god, then turned and saw Anna.

At the same moment, she kicked the door shut to muffle the report and squeezed the trigger. It was quite astonishingly easy.

He clutched at his stomach and collapsed, gasping, across the legs of his master.

A split second later Anna was out in the corridor. There was an open window, also the second Chinese. He came at her clumsily and Anna fired again. The bullet slowed but didn't stop him. Anna swung her legs over the

199

windowsill and let herself fall just as he grabbed at her. She heard material tear and landed in the flower-bed, minus half her dress but still firmly holding the beauty-box and the gun.

What had Precious Emerald said? South—across the mountains.

A whistle blew behind her, a searchlight stabbed the darkness. Anna hunched her shoulders and ran. The low huts near the airstrip came to life. Electric torches flickered. From the roof of the main building a sub-machine gun opened up. Bullets sprayed the ground a dozen yards to her right.

Anna jumped for the shadow of a clump of ornamental bushes.

A thousand yards away the mountains offered safety, hope, life. Between was the airstrip, open, as dangerous as a minefield, a place for capture, maiming and death.

Anna remembered for a second all the thousands of others, of dozens of nationalities, who had faced just this same situation. The prisoners of war on the run, the refugees between Hungary and Austria, the two Germanies, those who crossed the mined frontiers everywhere.

A strip of open ground, a gentle stroll under the stars. An innocent field. A wilderness of terror.

You could stay behind and no one would call you chicken. Or take the walk.

From the villa came an ear-splitting roar. Anna threw herself down and looked back. The whole building seemed to be bursting apart. Dust and debris began to rain down all about her. Glancing at her watch, she saw it was exactly ten minutes since she had escaped from the place. Screams and shouts came from the shambles. Anna saw some at least of the soldiers from the huts were now running towards what had been the villa.

Anna got to her feet and, very resolutely, started her walk across open ground under the stars and towards the hills.

Chapter Twenty

The Olympic Airways Comet from Athens to London touched down exactly on schedule.

The rather young, very serious Customs Officer looked at the sun-tanned girl before him with more than the usual amount of official curiosity. Around them jostled the returning holiday crowd, loaded with luggage and souvenirs, duty free drinks and cigarettes.

The Customs Officer looked at the girl's small, battered beauty-box. She seemed reluctant to let go of it, even for an instant.

'This is your only luggage, Miss?'

'Yes.'

'May I see your passport, please?'

Anna produced the American one, Anna O'Connor.

'Thank you.' He handed the passport back politely. 'Would you mind coming with me, please?'

Anna thought, 'Oh no!' To be stripped and searched now for heroin or something. That would be too much!

But she said, 'Why, certainly!' and followed the man.

The Officer opened the door of the examination-room and closed it again immediately, without entering.

Sarratt got up from the solitary chair, and smiled at her a crooked, embarrassed smile.

He said, 'You look a little older.'

'That's a hell of a way to say "hello" to a girl.' She opened the beauty-box and handed him the spools of tape. She said, 'I wouldn't in the least mind you searching me. But I don't like the atmosphere of the place. Here! The spoils of war. I suppose I could have sent them in the Diplomatic Bag from Athens. But I don't suppose you trust the Queen's Messengers?'

'I trust hardly anyone,' he said.

'I like the "hardly" bit. It suggests you're human after all.'

They had already spoken over scrambler phone, and he knew the gist of the story, and it occurred to her there had been really no need for him to meet her at all.

He said, 'How are you really?'

'Well, I've had a spot of gastro-enteritis, brought on by living on goat's milk, rather peculiar cheese, unwashed fruit and very rough wine up in the hills for three days. I like the men in that little army of irregulars. It's a marvellous outdoor life. If I were a man I'd join them.'

'You've seen the papers?'

'The plane crash?' Anna nodded. 'According to the *Giornale d'Italia* I bought in Rome, Nasser's navy have fished some of the wreckage out of the sea a few miles off Alexandria. But they're keeping very mum. No survivors. Those whom the god created, the god destroyed. I'd say undoubtedly a bomb.'

Sarratt nodded and lit a cigarette. He said, 'It's lucky you weren't on it.'

'Yes.' Anna turned before him. 'You like the dress? I owe the Chargé d'Affaires in Athens five hundred drachs for it. The poor man was very polite, very discreet. God knows what sort of riff-raff he thought I was.'

'It's very becoming,' he said. 'Green suits you.'

'In that case, how about taking me out to dinner?'

She noticed his hesitation, and added, 'It'll cost you nothing but money.'

'All right,' he said. 'I'd be honoured. Somewhere quiet?'

'And very English olde-worlde in the Thames Valley.'

Later, over the brandy, he relaxed, but still seemed preoccupied.

'Out with it,' she said. 'Tell me, *kicsi bárány*, are you worried about me?'

'No,' he said, 'I'm worried about the Minister.'

'But the dear man is having a wonderful self-important time settling the world's problems in Tirana,' Anna said.

'No,' Sarratt said. 'Just before I met you I got a flash from Albania. It seems the Minister's wife murdered her husband in their room last night.'

'Well, blow me down!' Anna said. 'And yesterday was the twenty-first.

'Yes.'

'The god's doing? For goodness sake, how?'

'Before she married the Minister,' Sarratt said, 'Mrs Hobbs was a missionary in China. Make what you can of that. I suppose, to be a hundred per cent efficient, *we* should have made something of it long ago.' He sighed heavily. 'The failure of a mission!'

'Well, cheer up,' Anna said. 'Thank God that's one place where even you can't butt in, when a man's alone with his wife in bed.'